STARSTRUCK

Cathy Hopkins lives in North London with her handsome husband and three deranged cats. Or is it the other way around – her handsome cats and deranged husband? She has had over twenty books published, including the six titles in the Mates, Dates series and the three titles in the Truth, Dare, Kiss or Promise series. Apart from that, she is looking for the answers to why we're here, where we've come from and what it's all about. She is also looking for the perfect hairdresser.

Also available from Piccadilly Press by Cathy Hopkins:

Mates, Dates and Inflatable Bras
Mates, Dates and Cosmic Kisses
Mates, Dates and Portobello Princesses
Mates, Dates and Sleepover Secrets
Mates, Dates and Sole Survivors
Mates, Dates and Mad Mistakes
Mates, Dates and Pulling Power
Truth, Dare, Kiss or Promise – White Lies and Barefaced Truths
Truth, Dare, Kiss or Promise – Pop Princess
Truth, Dare, Kiss or Promise – Teen Queens & Has-beens

Truth Dare

Kiss Promise

STARSTRUCK

Cathy Hopkins

PICCADILLY PRESS • LONDON

*Thanks as always to Brenda Gardner, Yasemin Uçar and the ever
fab team at Piccadilly Press. To Rosemary Bromley at Juvenilia.
To Steve Lovering for all his help and support. To Maff Potts for the low-
down on life as a runner on a film set. And to Steve Brenman,
Phil Howard Jones and Steve Denham for reminding me what
strange things adolescent boys can get up to!*

First published in Great Britain in 2003
by Piccadilly Press Ltd,
5 Castle Road, London NW1 8PR

A catalogue record for this book is available from
the British Library

ISBN: 1 85340 798 4 (trade paperback)

1 3 5 7 9 10 8 6 4 2

Printed and bound in Great Britain by Bookmarque Ltd
Typeset by Textype Typesetters
Cover design by Fielding Design
Set in 11.5/17.5pt Garamond

Polonious Plonker

'No way, Squidge,' said Becca. 'What do you think we are? Stupid?'

'No,' I replied. 'But why won't you do it?'

Lia, Cat, Becca, Mac and I were hanging out on the beach down at Whitsand Bay a couple of days before the Easter holidays. It was six in the evening; the light was perfect; there was no one around but us, and *all* I'd asked the girls to do was take their clothes off and pose naked against the rocks for me. OK, it might be a *bit* chilly, but apart from that, I couldn't see what the big deal was.

'Because you just want to cop a look at us naked, that's why,' said Becca.

'Do not,' I said. 'It's *art*. For my portfolio.' I wasn't lying. I needed to have a variety of pictures ready for when I went for college interviews. My plan is to study film technique, as my ambition is to be a director, and having a good selection of photo stills to show at interviews is essential. Not that what Becca had said wasn't also true. Course I wanted to see the girls naked. I'm a sixteen-year-old boy, and in my opinion, Lia, Cat and Becca are the best looking girls at our school. I'd be mad *not* to want to see them naked.

Cat turned to Mac. 'I notice you're staying very quiet. What do you think?'

Mac gave her a cheeky grin. 'I think you should definitely do it. For *art*.'

'Yeah right,' said Cat. 'And what exactly is your contribution going to be?'

'Appreciation,' Mac replied. 'Art needs an audience.'

Lia burst out laughing. 'You just want to see us naked too.'

'You bet,' said Mac.

Suddenly, Becca got up from where she'd been sitting on the sand and came to stand in front of me with her hands on her hips. 'OK,' she said. 'I will if you will.'

'What do you mean?'

'If you and Mac strip off, we will too.'

'Speak for yourself,' said Cat.

'Yeah,' said Lia. 'Don't include us.'

'Look,' I said. 'All I want is for you to curl up against the rocks. You'll have your backs to me. I don't want a Page-Three pose or anything. My shots *will* be artistic. See, it's all about shapes and textures.'

Cat cracked up laughing. 'Nice try, Squidge. Not heard that one before. Oo, all about shapes and textures. Now get your kit off.'

I sat down on the rock behind me and gazed out to sea. Today was turning out to be a bit of a let down. It was my birthday. It was supposed to be fun, a celebration, but I was fast learning the meaning of the saying that goes: 'Blessed is he who has no expectations, for he is not disappointed.' Too true, judging by today. Sweet sixteen, that's me. Only I don't feel sweet. I feel crap.

I'd got up this morning full of expectations. As you do on your birthday. Down to brekkie, expecting the works: a fry-up, my favourite, even though it was a school day; presents laid out on the kitchen table; cards . . . But no. There was nothing. No one had even made me a cup of tea. Dad had already left to do a road rescue for some bloke stranded on the A38 and Mum was with one of her customers – old Mrs McNelly from down the road – doing a quick rinse and blow-dry. Cat says my parents are the most important people in the village because Dad's the only mechanic for miles and Mum's the only hairdresser. I guess Cat's right, but it can be a bit boring some days, like this one, when you want a bit of their attention for yourself for a change. At least my little sister, Amy, acknowledged my big day. As soon as I entered the kitchen, she chucked her beaker at me. She's only two. It's her way of saying 'Hi'. Unfortunately it was full of milk, which splattered all over my T-shirt.

'Your dad said he'd catch you later,' said Janice. (She's Amy's childminder and my cousin.) 'Happy birthday, kid.'

And that was it. That and the three cards on the table: a flowery one from Gran, one with a boy and his dog sitting on a pier from Auntie Bea and from my kid brother, Will – a Christmas card with the word 'Christmas' crossed out and Birthday written in instead. I couldn't complain. He'd learned that little trick from me, along with wrapping presents up in newspaper – you can make them look arty farty if you add a bit of coloured ribbon. From my parents, zilch. And there was me thinking that sixteen was one of the big birthdays. As in sixteen, eighteen, twenty-one, thirty, forty etc. Big day. Special day. One to be acknowledged. Obviously I'd got it wrong. Anyway, I told myself to get a life, and set off for school.

School was school. No big deal. No special birthday announcements at assembly or being given the day off, but then I was hardly expecting that, was I? At least my mates and my girlfriend, Lia, hadn't forgotten. We got together at break and they gave me their pressies, plus Lia had brought a flask of hot chocolate and a carrot cake with lemon butter-icing. (My favourite.) Really nice. Cat and Becca had clubbed together and got me a Red Hot Chili Peppers CD, Mac got me a DVD of the uncut version of *Reservoir Dogs* and Becca had also got me some fancy soap. (Is she trying to say something? I wondered. Better check the old armpit aroma.)

After we'd stuffed ourselves with cake, Lia gave me her present: the most amazing photography book. One of those enormous heavy ones that cost a fortune. It's by a guy called Bill Brandt. The shots are black and white and grainy. All the photos are of landscapes, at least that's what you think at first. When you look closer, you realise that a rock is actually the curve of someone's bum or their shoulder, a piece of driftwood is actually an arm or a leg. It's the way he arranges things then puts the light on them. As I said, it's all shapes and textures. Totally brilliant. Course, I couldn't wait to have a go myself, but I soon found out that getting people, even your best mates, to pose nude is not the easiest of tasks. I decided to try once more before giving up.

'Oh come on,' I said, turning back to my friends. 'I'm not giving you a line just to get you naked. Honest. And who else can I ask?'

'Ask Mac,' said Becca with a grin.

'Too skinny. Not got the right curves,' I said. 'Girls make better shapes. So, please. It would be so cool if I could get these shots and no one would ever know it was you.'

'What's the point then?' asked Becca.

Typical Becca, I thought. She loves being the centre of attention and even though she's objecting to posing, I know that part of her would love it, just to be able to tell people in a gallery, 'That's meee in that photo!'

'Point is,' I replied, 'I get some great shots for my portfolio that are a bit different. Point is, they may help me get into college and out of here.'

'Why do you want to get out of here?' asked Lia, indicating the shoreline stretching out for miles on either side of us. 'This place is heaven.'

'Not when you've lived here your whole life,' I said. 'Not when you've photographed every inch of the place, every nook, cranny, tree, rock, person . . . There's a whole world out there beyond Cornwall. I can't wait to start exploring it.'

I looked into the distance to where Lia had pointed. No doubt, this area is beautiful. The coast on the south side of the peninsula is totally unspoilt, just beach, sand and cliff as far as the eye can see. Yeah, impressive. But sometimes lately, I feel like I don't see it anymore. I feel suffocated here. Like in the village, everyone knows everyone; they all know each other's business. Lia's relatively new to the area. Only been down here a year. She still sees it with fresh eyes.

Becca stood in front of me. 'Did you hear me, Squidge? I said, I'll strip if you will. You in, Lia?'

Lia looked up at me from where she was sitting on the sand. 'I'll think about it. Maybe.'

I looked at Mac. He shrugged. 'It'd be a laugh,' he said. 'You?'

An image of Lia naked suddenly flashed through my mind . . . I shook my head. 'Forget it,' I muttered. 'I'll find someone who will pose without a list of conditions.'

Becca tossed her head. 'Suit yourself. Once in a lifetime offer.'

'My loss then,' I said and put my camera back in my rucksack. I couldn't risk it. If I had to take my clothes off at the same time as the girls, who knows what would happen. In the trouser department, that is. Just thinking about it was enough sometimes. It's been hell these last few years. My willie seems to have developed a life of its own, and has been known to stand to attention at the most inappropriate times.

It's so weird. It's like having a little animal with a mind of its own living on your body. Sometimes, there's nothing I can do to stop it. I have control over every other part of my body – arms, legs, hands, feet – none of them move involuntarily, only if I will it. Not the old fella though. He has his own agenda. Sometimes (especially when there are girls around), no matter how hard I try to will him to stay down he takes no notice. So . . . Lia, who I fancy like mad, in the nude; Becca and Cat in the nude; me in the nude; me and my friend (and I don't mean Mac here), displayed for all the world to see . . . Can't risk it. Nope. No way.

Girls don't know how lucky they are. If they get turned on, or whatever, who's to know? They can keep it secret. But for boys it's different. When we first start noticing the girlie bits of girls – a glimpse of boob, a hint of thigh – wahey, Polonius Plonker is up and ready for action, with his silent salute to all things feminine. So, no. Me getting naked at the same time as the girls was not an option. Anyway, I had another idea for a shot.

'How about we try something else?' I said. 'Won't take a mo.' Looking at Becca's hair glinting in the evening sun had given me the idea. She has the most amazing long, red hair. Not ginger, but red. Titian red.

'What?' asked Becca.

'How about you all lie on the beach in a line close together,' I said, 'then splay your hair out around you.'

'Not got much hair to splay out since I had it chopped,'

said Cat, flinging herself out on the sand. 'But I can do the lying down bit.'

Lia lay next to her, then Becca.

'And you at the end Mac,' I said as he lay down at the end of the line.

'And you're going to photograph what?' asked Mac. 'Our heads? Our profiles? What?'

'Your hair. Tops of your heads. It will be a shot of textures.' I said kneeling down, then lying so that I had the right angle. All the colours looked great through the camera viewfinder. Cat's short, dark mop was a nice contrast to Lia's hair, which is long and white-blond – beautiful, like water or silk. Next to her blond hair was Becca's, the colour of blood in the evening light. Then at the end of the line, Mac's blond spikes. From the right angle, the combination of their hair looked like some alien landscape. An hour or so in the dark room and I could crop off their faces and focus just on the hair. Yeah, the finished effect would look cool. Not Bill Brandt, but different.

'Looks really good,' I said, as I moved around, firing off a reel of film. 'Yeah, thanks. Great. That's it.'

'Can we get up now?' asked Cat, after I'd shot from every angle I thought might work.

'Yeah, thanks, guys,' I said. 'That looked brilliant.'

'Good, because I'm starving,' said Becca, getting up and

heading for the steps back up the cliff. 'Neeed foooooood.' She glanced at her watch. 'Ohmigod, it's late. God. Got to go. Coming Mac?'

Mac scrambled up to follow her. 'Yeah, sure,' he said.

'What's the hurry?' I asked.

'Nothing,' said Mac. 'Just said I'd be back at a reasonable time tonight. Supper. Homework. Cat? Lia? You guys coming?'

'Yeah. Sorry, Squidge, got to go,' said Cat. 'You coming?'

'Later,' I said. 'I might get some more shots before the sun disappears.'

Cat got up to go with Mac and Becca, but first she looked at me with concern. 'Sorry about the nudie shots, Squidge.'

'S'OK,' I said. 'I know millions of people who'll pose naked. No problemo.'

Actually, I reckon I could get Cat to pose if I could get her on her own. I've seen her naked before. OK, maybe not since we were five, but so what? I'm sure she wouldn't mind if the others weren't here. We've known each other all our lives and been mates since as long as I can remember. We went out for a while, years in fact, then suddenly it seemed pointless, like dating your sister or something. She felt the same way. Now she fancies Lia's brother, Ollie. She seems pretty happy on the occasions when he comes down here from his boarding school in London. I hope he doesn't mess her around too much. I don't know him that well, but he seems like he could be a user, given half a chance.

As Cat, Becca and Mac headed back up the cliff, Lia watched them anxiously.

'We ought to get going as well, don't you think?' she asked.

'No hurry,' I said. My birthday wasn't over yet and it could still turn out well given half an hour alone with the most stunning girl in Cornwall.

Lia looked at her watch. She clearly didn't share my enthusiasm. 'No, really, Squidge. It will be dark soon.'

'Not for ages,' I said, 'and don't worry, I'll ride home with you.'

'No, let's go now. But . . . can I come back to yours first? I . . . I, er, want to borrow that book you've got on the Tudors for my history essay. Dad can pick me up from your house later.'

I shrugged. 'Sure. If that's what you really want.'

Lia nodded. 'Anyway, it's your birthday. Won't your parents have organised something for you? A special birthday supper or something?'

I shook my head. 'Nah, doesn't look like it. I suppose it's my own fault really. Mum kept asking for weeks, "Squidge, what would you like to do on your birthday?" And I kept saying, "Oh, nothing. Don't make a fuss."' I didn't want to make a big deal of it to Lia, as her family is loaded, but money's been tight for Mum and Dad since Amy appeared on the scene. And Will will be going to secondary school in September so he'll need loads of new stuff. I was trying to make it easier for them. You know – don't mind me, I don't need big birthday gestures. Funny though, because now it actually is my birthday, I would have liked them to do something.

Lia put her hand on my arm and gave it a squeeze. 'I'm so sorry, Squidge. I wish you'd told me; I'd have sorted something for this evening but . . . I do have to get back home soon after I've picked up the book.'

We sat for a few moments, holding hands and gazing out at the ocean. This is my favourite time of day. It's so still. It's the time when you get the best light as well. I decided to get my camera out and take a few last shots of Lia. We've been going out for just over a month now and I still can't quite believe my luck. Lia Axford, *my* girlfriend. She's not just the best looking girl in Cornwall, I reckon she may be the best looking girl in the whole world. I totally fell for her the first moment I saw her in the school corridor last September. Long, blond hair, silver-blue eyes, tall, slim: a top babe, a ten – no, an eleven – out of ten. I thought she was way out of my league and never thought she'd look at me twice. But she did. We've had a great few weeks. But she's been kind of distant the last few days. And now she seems distracted, like she doesn't want to be here. She seems edgy and she keeps looking at her watch. Maybe she's gone off me because I asked the other girls to pose naked. Maybe she's jealous. Maybe she's got bored. Only one way to find out if she's still into me, I thought and leaned over to kiss her.

She pulled away and looked at her watch again. 'We really ought to get going,' she said. Then she got up and began heading for the steps.

'OK. Fine,' I said and started packing away my stuff. I know not to push it with girls when they're not in the mood. But something is definitely going on with her, I thought as I followed her across the beach. She clearly doesn't want to be on her own with me. I felt a sinking feeling in my stomach. Maybe she didn't want to go out with me any more. Inevitable I suppose. A girl like Lia could have anyone: she's lived in London; her dad's a famous rock star; her family are mega rich. (They live in a mansion on a private estate, while my family live in a fisherman's cottage in the village.) Why should a girl like her be interested in a backwater boy like me?

When we got to the foot of the steps leading up the cliff, she suddenly turned back to me. 'Hey, remember last summer? We played truth, dare, kiss or promise here for the first time?' I nodded. 'OK, so truth, dare, kiss or promise?' she asked.

'Well I'm not going to say dare as you'll make me do something mad, like run into the sea with all my clothes on. Not kiss, as I don't want to kiss anyone else but you. Truth, you know everything about me so . . . So it looks like it's the last option – promise.'

'OK,' she said. 'OK . . . Promise.' She thought for a moment. 'I think the most important thing in any relationship – whether you're friends, boyfriend and girlfriend, whatever – is telling the truth about how you really feel. So. Promise. Promise to tell the truth, even if it hurts, no matter what, and I will as well . . .'

'Yeah, course. We should tell each other the truth about how we really feel,' I said. 'Promise.'

Just at that moment, her mobile rang. 'Won't be a mo,' she said. She pulled her phone out of the back pocket of her jeans then walked a few steps ahead, away from me. She was talking really quietly, like she didn't want me to hear.

Oh, here it comes, I thought. She's going to dump me, I know it. Promise to tell the truth about how we really feel, she'd said. And, by her behaviour of late, she'd been feeling disinterested. So prepare yourself pal, I thought. You're going to get dumped. Huh, on my birthday, too. The sinking feeling in my stomach felt like *Titanic*.

'Who were you talking to?' I asked when she came back to join me a few moments later.

'Oh, no one,' she said, blushing slightly. 'I mean, just Mum wanting to know where we . . . where *I* was. I said I wouldn't be long and that I was going back to your house for a moment.'

She was lying. I could tell. Sometimes I don't get girls, I thought. She just came out with that promise thing about how important it is to tell each other the truth. Then two seconds later, someone phones up and Lia tells a blatant lie about who it is. I don't get it. I decided not to confront her though. I didn't really want to know who it was on the phone, in case it was some guy who's been waiting next in line to replace me and his number just came up. Who knows? Maybe it was Jonno Appleton. She went out with him for a while earlier this year. Maybe he's back on the scene. But then maybe it's someone from when she was at school up in London; she must have loads of admirers there that I don't even know about. Whoever it was, I reckoned I was history. She was hurrying up the cliff side like she couldn't stand to be in my company another minute.

'The sun will be going down soon,' I said, running to catch her up. 'Let's stay and watch.'

Lia couldn't get away fast enough and carried on towards

the top. 'No. Let's go. Um, I'm cold. And hungry. Aren't you hungry, Squidge? Come on.'

That was it. It was over between Lia and I. Ah well, I tried to tell myself, it was good while it lasted. I just wished that it had lasted longer between us. A lot longer.

Make 'Em Laugh

2

LIA WAS abnormally quiet as we whizzed back down through the lanes to the village on our bikes. I guess I was too. I felt very sad. I thought we had something special going. I thought she really liked me.

'Is something the matter?' I asked, as I rode round the back of our house and parked outside the garage.

'Course not,' said Lia, sliding off her bike. But she still looked uncomfortable and she checked her watch again. Was she meeting someone later? I wondered. If so, who?

I opened the back door to the kitchen and switched on the light. No one home. I hadn't really expected that there would be. Tuesday night was Mum's girlie night with some of the other mums in the village. It was also Will's Scout night, and Dad would probably be where he is most nights after work: down the pub. A tiny part of me had hoped that they might have made a surprise supper, but no. My own fault, I reminded myself. You told them not to make a fuss.

'The book you want is in the front room,' I said, when we got into the hall. 'It's in the bookcase, near the top, I think. You go on in. I've got to go to the bathroom.'

Actually, I wanted a few moments alone to compose myself. To get ready for Lia to give me the bad news. My second time being dumped. Sort of. With Cat it was mutual, really. Still, not nice. Not easy.

I went into the bathroom, closed the door and stared at myself in the mirror. Maybe I'm not good-looking enough for her, I thought, as I stared at my reflection. I know I'm not Brad Pitt, with the chiselled jaw and the blue, blue eyes, but I'm not bad looking either. Neither good nor bad: sort of in the middle, I reckon. Five foot eight, brown hair, brown eyes, no spots – that's got to be a plus, some guys in our year are plagued with them. And Cat always used to tell me that I was cute looking. That's something, I guess. But anyway, I told myself, looks aren't supposed to be as important to girls as they are to boys. I read in one of Cat's girlie magazines that top of most girls' 'what I find attractive in a boy' list is a sense of humour. Yeah, that's it, I thought. I should do something to make Lia laugh. Maybe I've been too serious lately. Yeah, maybe I've been a bit heavy, always talking about how I wanted to get out of

Cornwall and what a backwater it was. Maybe she's bored with me droning on, when she's so happy to be down here. Yeah, I have to lighten up. I have to make her laugh. But how? I racked my brains for something funny. Tell her jokes? Do impersonations of the teachers at our school? No. Do some of my mad dancing? I had a whole repertoire – Hawaiian, Spanish, Russian, disco, go-go and alien. One of those usually got her cracking up.

Then I had a better idea.

I crept into Will's room and rooted around in the bottom of his cupboard until I found what I was looking for. Yes, there they were, in a bin bag behind his smelly trainers. Enormous plastic boobs. We were in a fancy dress shop in Plymouth with Dad about three weeks ago and we bought them ready to make Mum laugh on April Fool's Day. I quickly stripped down to my boxers and strapped the boobs on. Then into Mum's room and a quick look at her wig collection. She keeps loads of them for people to try on when they don't know how they want their hair cut. Yes, a long, blond, curly one, I think. A quick rustle around at the top of her wardrobe and I found the pink feather boa she keeps for dressing up occasions. What else? Shoes? No, Dad's wellies. I pulled them out from his side of the wardrobe and stuck my feet into them. Hmm, sexy – not. I checked my appearance in the mirror and added a quick smudge of red lipstick to complete the look. Yes, this could work. I was even making myself laugh, I looked so ridiculous.

I crept down the stairs to the front room and listened at the door. The room was quiet. I hoped Lia hadn't done a runner, come over all cowardly and next thing I know there's a text message telling me that it's all over. No, she wouldn't do that, I thought. She's just in there wondering how to word it. So. This was my last chance. If this didn't get her laughing, nothing would.

I flung open the door and wiggled my false chest into the room. 'Tadaaaa . . .'

But where was Lia? It was dark in there. I heard a click and light flooded the room.

'ARGHH!' I screamed, as twenty or so voices shouted, 'SURPRISE!'

I don't know who was more shocked – me or them. Heads appeared from behind the sofa, from behind the curtains, from under the table. Half the village was in there, hiding in our front room. There was Mrs Wells from the post office, Mrs McNelly from down the road. *All* my relatives: Auntie Bea, Auntie Pat, Auntie Celia, Uncle John, Uncle Louis, Uncle David, Uncle Bill, Uncle Ed, Cousin Roger, Cousin Arthur. Mum, Dad, Will, Amy and . . . Oh hell . . . Gran. She looked a bit startled! And

Cat, Mac, Becca and Lia, who were killing themselves laughing. Becca had to hold Mac up, he was laughing so hard. I started to bounce out of the room backwards but then they all started singing 'Happy Birthday'.

All I wanted to do was get upstairs and get some proper clothes on, but how could I do that when everyone was singing to me. I bent over, crossed my legs and put my hands over my crotch, and tried to grin like I was enjoying it. But talk about embarrassment. This moment gets the prize.

At last the singing stopped.

'Nice one,' said Will, indicating my boobs and Kermit the Frog boxers. 'That how you impress the birds?'

'Works for me,' said Lia, coming forward and slipping her hand into mine. 'Happy Birthday, Squidge.'

'So . . . you're not . . . um, you're not going to dump me? I thought that maybe after that game of truth, dare, kiss or promise, and you saying we had to be honest about our feelings, you meant it was time to call it a day.'

Lia looked confused for a moment. 'Dump you? No *way*. Why would I? We've only just started going out.'

Then the penny dropped. 'It was your job to get me here on time, wasn't it? That's why you were acting so weird?'

Lia nodded. 'Yeah. Sorry about that. Your mum phoned when we were down at the beach and said to get you here fast. Some of the old dears were eating all the crisps and there weren't going to be any left for you. But, er,' she looked me up and down, 'talking about acting weird, anything you'd like to say about your outfit?'

'Yes,' said Mum, coming over to join us. 'Is there something you want to tell us?'

'I . . . I wanted to make Lia laugh.'

'Mission accomplished, I'd say,' said Mum then she looked at my wig. 'Though next time, go for the brunette wig – I don't think blond is really your colour.'

Suddenly I felt a large hand on my shoulder. 'Here, Squidge, lad,' said Dad. 'Come and open your presents.'

'Give me a sec,' I said, backing out of the room. 'Got to change into . . . er something . . . you know, put some clothes on.' I raced upstairs, flung off the wig, wiped off the lipstick, put on my jeans and T-shirt then belted back down the stairs again.

On the table was a pile of presents. Brilliant. One of them in particular caught my attention. It was wrapped in our traditional Squires family style: newspaper tied up with bright red ribbon.

'Nice job,' I said to Will, as I made my way over to the table. Everyone stood round while I ripped off the paper. Dad beamed at me when I saw what was in the package.

'Is that the one you wanted?' he asked.

I nodded. I was speechless. It was a camcorder. A Sony Digicam. The latest model. Way beyond Mum and Dad's budget. 'But Dad . . . you can't . . .'

'Can and did,' said Dad, tapping the side of his nose. 'No worries. Cousin Ed got it for me. Special deal for family. So don't you go thinking about the cost or anything. It's your sixteenth birthday and we wanted you to have what you wanted.'

I laughed. Our family – they're more like a tribe. There are hundreds of us: aunts, uncles, cousins, second cousins . . . third cousins. We inhabit the whole village and twenty miles around. If anyone ever needs anything doing or fixing or fetching, one of the Squires family will be able to arrange it.

At that moment, the lights went out again and Mum came in carrying a cake with sixteen lit candles. Everyone started singing 'Happy Birthday' again. Even Amy, who was on Gran's lap, tried to join in with a squeal.

'Blow them out and make a wish,' said Mum as she set the cake down in front of me on the table.

It had been decorated to look like a camera. (It was probably done by Auntie Celia – she runs the bakery.) I looked around at all the smiling faces. This is an ace birthday, I thought, as I closed my eyes and wondered what to wish for.

I smiled to myself. My family is great. All these people here tonight are great. My mates are great. My girlfriend is great . . . so what more to wish for? My life is good. I know what to expect so . . . I wish . . . I wish for something new. I wish for the unexpected.

Then I took a deep breath and blew.

Tales of the Unexpected

3

MY *OWN* camcorder. My own, as in not borrowed, mine. I was so chuffed, I wanted to sleep with it next to me on my pillow. I guess I'd been lucky until then as I'd always had the use of one. Well, part-time at least. Mr Cook, my art teacher, had let me borrow the school one at weekends and in the holidays, if no one else had booked it first. He's really cool and he knows that I'm serious about getting into the film business. Always have been. He also knows that I always look after any equipment and I'd never let him down. But now, I had my own. I didn't have to sign release slips to take out the school one. I didn't have to share it with Mark Atman in the sixth form or Trish Donelan in Year Ten, who are also film enthusiasts. So T.T. Totally Top.

The day after my birthday, I got up at six o'clock and went down to Cawsand beach to try it out. I was hoping to get some shots of what it's like there early in the morning, with the village slowly coming to life around the cove. This particular morning, however, the atmosphere was sadly lacking. Clouds hung heavy in the sky, threatening rain, and there wasn't much light. There would be better mornings, I decided, and I headed for home and a bit of breakfast before school.

And that's when it happened.

I was charging up the stairs, two at a time, when I missed my footing or slipped or something. It happened so fast. I fell back, just managing to twist myself around so that I wasn't falling backwards. Without thinking, I put my arms out so that I didn't land face first and bust my nose open. And then there I was, a crumpled heap at the bottom of the stairs. I soon saw what had happened: I'd slipped on one of Amy's teddy bears. It was on the stairs and I hadn't seen it.

Mum's face appeared over the banister upstairs in the hall. 'What's the commotion?' she asked, then she saw me lying there. 'Are you all right?'

I got up and shook it off. 'Yeah. Nothing broken.'

'What happened?'

'Slipped on Amy's teddy bear.'

Mum rolled her eyes. 'That child is a health hazard. Sure you're OK?'

I nodded.

'Good. Put the kettle on then. I'll be down in a mo.'

I went into the kitchen and got my video camera out of my rucksack to check it wasn't damaged. I was pretty sure it wouldn't be as they're built robustly these days, but I could see immediately that something wasn't right. I held it up to the window and looked through it. My heart sank. The view through the lens looked distorted.

As I heard Mum's footsteps on the stairs, I quickly put the camera back in my rucksack. I didn't want to worry her until I was certain it was broken. It might be something; it might be nothing, but no point in ruining her day, too.

'Sometimes you have to be careful what you wish for,' I said to Mac, when I met up with him in the lunch-break at school. 'Unexpected doesn't necessarily mean unexpected in a fun, good way. No, unexpected can mean a complete, utter and absolute disaster.'

'What are you on about?' he asked.

'The unexpected. That's what I wished for when I blew out my birthday candles.'

He nodded. 'Right. So what's happened then?'

'Worst thing that possibly could – I broke my new camera falling down the stairs. Me, Squidge, who has used cameras since he was ten – rolled on beaches with them, hung off cliffs with them, scrambled over rocks with them and never dropped one of them, not once. Then I get a fabola new, state of the art camcorder, and talullah, what do I do? I trip over a teddy bear that Amy has left on the stairs, go flying, crash down on to the floor, the tiled floor, I may add, and . . . *kaput*.'

'How bad is it?'

'Not sure. But I have a good idea.'

'We could go to that place in Torpoint that fixes cameras,' said Mac. 'I'll come with you.'

'Can't. My cousin Jo works there,' I said. 'It would get back to Dad or Cousin Ed. I can't go anywhere local with it. Not with the tribe on every corner. That's the downside of having family everywhere.' Yeah, I thought, they might be able to do a deal on anything, fix anything, get things sorted, but when you want something done on the quiet, you've got to travel, or else word will spread like the Asian flu.

'So what are you going to do?' Mac asked.

'Go to Plymouth,' I said. 'I have to go somewhere no one will know me.'

After an agonisingly long day at school, I set off with Mac to find a quiet photographic shop in Plymouth.

'Sorry mate, the lens is damaged,' said a man in a shop we found in the Old Town.

'But can it be fixed?' I asked. 'It's really important.'

The man looked again at the camera lens. 'Maybe, but it wouldn't be cheap. For what it would cost, you might as well get a new one.'

'And how much would that cost?' I asked, mentally totting up the dosh I had stashed away from my paper rounds.

'Four hundred pounds.'

I am a dead man, I thought. How will I ever be able to tell Mum and Dad?

I left the shop and went to look for Mac, who had taken off to another street to buy some oil pastels from an artist's supply shop. He wants to be a cartoonist when he leaves school. I reckon he might make a name for himself – he's good. He can paint, draw, do illustrations, but really cartooning is his thing. He can capture anyone with just a few strokes of his pen. Takes talent, that does. You need an eye for the absolute essentials. It's a bit like photography, you have to have an eye for that too. It's one of the things we have in common as mates. We might go to the same college if we can find one that does film studies as well as cartooning and animation.

I crossed the road and as I went round the corner, I spotted Mac looking in the window of the art shop. He looked up and beckoned me over to him.

'Hey, come and look at this,' he said, then he saw my face. 'Not good news?'

I shook my head. 'Think I'm going to need a small miracle this time. It'll cost a fortune to fix. Guy in the shop said I may as well get a new one, but no way can I afford one and I can't go to Cousin Ed or Jo to get it repaired, as word will get back to Dad.'

'Maybe you should just bite the bullet and tell him,' said Mac. 'Accidents happen. He'll understand, won't he?'

'Yeah,' I said. 'And that's exactly why I *don't* want to tell him. Him being understanding would make it even worse. I know Mum and Dad really went out on a limb to get me that camcorder. I don't want to disappoint them. Let them down like a stupid kid who breaks his toy on Christmas morning. No, what I'll do is get a Saturday job. I'll work in the Easter holidays. I'll sort it.'

Mac started grinning like an idiot.

'It's not funny, Mac.'

'I know. I'm not smiling because of that. I'm smiling because someone up there must be looking after you.'

'Yeah right. And where exactly were they when I tripped over Rupert the Bear?'

'Look in the window,' said Mac.

'What at?' I asked.

'At the notices,' said Mac pointing to a noticeboard on

the left of the window. 'One small miracle, I do believe.'

There were loads of notices on postcards: flat to rent; bicycle for sale; cleaner needed.

'What?' I asked. 'You suggesting I leave home and become a cleaner? I suppose I could sell my bike. Yeah. I guess that's an option . . .'

Mac shook his head and pointed to a notice to the left of the others. 'There, you dufus.'

Then I saw it.

Ever wanted to work in the movies? Now is your chance.
Needed: extras, drivers, runners, cleaners, caterers.
Must be local.
Must be available between April 14th and May 5th.
Want to know more? Call 07365 88921 and ask for Sandra.

The answer to my prayers, I thought. 'That's in the Easter holidays,' I gasped. 'I wonder where exactly they're going to film.'

I turned to Mac, but he was already on his mobile asking for someone called Sandra.

4   *Interview*

'TRANSPORT?'

'Yes, I have a bike,' I replied.

'Mobile?'

'Yes, I am. I also have a mobile phone.' I was in Millbrook in a tiny office that the film's production team had hired for a couple of days to use for interviewing staff for the shoot.

The guy doing the interview gave me a 'don't try to be clever with me' look. 'Availability?'

'Twenty-four hours a day for the three weeks over Easter.' I meant it too. I was keen. Double keen. The chance to work in the movies was a dream come true for me.

My interviewer didn't look that old. Maybe early twenties. Whatever, he sure was full of himself. He was leaning back in his chair, wearing a pair of Police sunglasses, even though we were inside and it was a gloomy day. I guess he thought it made him look cool. I thought it made him look like a dick. He'd introduced himself as Roland, third production assistant (whatever that meant). Licence to arse around like he was somebody – that much was clear. Still, no matter. I could put up with eejits like him if it meant the chance to work as part of a film crew for a few weeks.

Talk of the production had spread through the village the same day that Mac and I had seen the advertisement, and everyone was up for getting involved in some way. The production to be filmed was *Great Expectations*. Some guy I'd never heard of – Charlie Bennett – was directing and the producer was Jason Harwood. Apprently it was a musical version of the book. Sounded a bit naff to me, and personally I don't think anyone will ever top David Lean's version but I wasn't going to argue. Naff or not, this was happening on my doorstep. Nothing as exciting had happened in this area since five years ago, when Tom Cruise was spotted in a B&B in Kingsand. Allegedly – I still don't believe it was him. But this was for definite.

News of the production was buzzing all round school on the last day of term and everyone wanted to be in on the action. Holiday jobs were a rarity round our way, particularly before the summer season began in mid-May, so the chance to earn some extra cash earlier in the year was an opportunity not to be missed. Cat and Becca had already been down to the makeshift office in Millbrook and signed up to be washer-uppers and helpers in the catering trailers. And both had got a promise that they could be extras in any crowd scenes. Mac wasn't going to miss out on his chance of earning some extra dosh, either, and had got himself hired as car-washer for two days a week. Me, I wanted to get right into the heart of it. I wanted to be a runner.

'What do you know about the book?' asked Roland.

'Dickens classic. There have been many film versions but I still reckon David Lean's is the best.'

'Why?'

'He was the master of lighting.'

'Yes, I guess,' said Roland. 'And Robert de Niro is brilliant as Magwitch.'

'That was the later version. The one with Gwyneth Paltrow.'

'Yeah. So?'

'In David Lean's version, Magwitch was played by Finlay Currie. Jean Simmons played Estella as a child and Valerie Hobson played her as an older woman.'

'Quite the little know it all, aren't you?'

'Not really.'

'Age?'

'Sixteen.'

Roland peered over his shades. 'You're wasting my time, kid,' he said, as he pushed the glasses back up his nose.

'Pardon?'

'You heard me.'

I didn't like this guy but I was determined to stay polite. 'And why might I be wasting your time?'

'Runners have to be eighteen.'

'Where does it say that?'

Roland pointed to his chest. 'It's me who's doing the hiring here.'

'Yeah, and you wouldn't regret giving me this chance. I know this area like the back of my hand. Know everyone. Have bike will travel.' I gave him what I hoped was my most winning smile.

'Next,' he called and turned away to make a phone call.

I was dismissed. So much for my first job interview. Fired before I'd been hired.

'Oh bad luck,' said Lia. I'd arrived at her house an hour later and told her the whole story. 'We're in the kitchen. Come and meet, er . . . Mum's friend.'

'Yeah, major bummer,' I said, as I followed her through. 'Lesson number one in going for jobs: never let on that you know more than the dufus who's doing the hiring. Oh, hi, Mrs Axford.'

Mrs Axford was sitting on a stool at the counter, chatting with another woman about the same age as her. 'What's that?' she said, looking up. 'You didn't get the job? Why not?'

'Squidge knew more about the film than the guy doing the hiring,' said Lia. 'He thought Robert De Niro was in David Lean's version of *Great Expectations*.'

'I wasn't trying to be smart or anything,' I said. 'Although the guy was a bit of a prat. I was just stating the facts: Magwich was played by Finlay Currie in the Lean version.'

Mrs Axford's friend raised an eyebrow as though I'd said something amusing.

'Exactly,' said Mrs Axford, beckoning me to sit next her friend. 'Sit down. Meet a friend of mine from London. Mrs – '

'You can call me Charlotte,' interrupted her friend, in a husky voice. She looked nice. Attractive. Shoulder-length red hair. Slim. Probably an ex-model like Lia's mum – she had the same cut-glass cheekbones.

'And I'm Squidge,' I said.

'Interesting nickname,' she said.

'We call him Squidge because he's always looking through a camera with his eye squidged up,' said Lia.

'Partly that. And also because my name is Squires, Jack Squires, so the nickname came easy. Squires – Squidge . . .'

'Sounds like you're interested in movies, Squidge,' said Charlotte, looking at me closely.

'And some. I want to be a film director one day. That's why it's a real pisser – sorry, I mean bummer – that I didn't get the job.'

'And why didn't you?'

'Guy hiring said runners had to be eighteen.'

'Oh did he?' said Charlotte. 'I've never heard that before.'

'Neither have I. I don't think he liked me. It was one of those classic, hate-at-first-sight scenarios.'

'Well that's a shame,' said Mrs Axford, 'because you'd have been brilliant. No one knows this area better than you.'

'That's what I tried to tell him,' I said. 'Bummer, huh?'

Charlotte smiled. 'Yeah, as you say, bummer. And it sounds like they could do with someone like you around. Someone who knows the area. I . . . er, I read that they've run into trouble finding locations already. Apparently they need a place for the scene where Magwitch leaps out on the young Pip at the beginning. Some deserted graveyard maybe.'

'The one on the way up to Rame Head would be perfect,' I said. 'It's overgrown and spooky up there. But David Lean used a graveyard in his version. They ought to use somewhere different. I know where! The ruin out at Penlee

Point would be better. Brilliant in fact. It would be a great hiding place for Magwitch as no one can see the ruin from the road or the top of the cliff. Even some of the locals don't know that it's there. Yeah, and it would make sense as the sea's down below and Magwitch was supposed to have escaped from a ship carrying prisoners. It's all rocky and deserted out there. Plus in the mornings, it's often good and misty round that side of the peninsula. It would be really atmospheric if the light was right.'

Charlotte looked at me steadily for a few moments and I felt myself beginning to blush. I wasn't used to this kind of attention from older women.

'I can see film really is your passion,' she said.

I nodded. 'Yeah. And locations are such a hugely important part of it. That and the light. That's what I love about film. Unlike video, where what you see through the lens is what you get, you never know with film until it comes back from the lab. The light can change. You send your film off to be processed and bite your nails until you get it back. God, I wish I was doing locations on this movie. There are so many brilliant ones down here but you have to know where to go and at what time of day to get them at their best.' Suddenly I felt self-conscious. Charlotte was still staring at me. I'd probably got a bit carried away, rabbiting on without drawing breath. I can do that when I get going about film making.

'Er, Squidge,' she started to say, looking at her watch. 'Oops! Got to get moving. I've got a million things to do.' She got out her mobile and dialled a number, listened then sighed. 'It's switched off. What a nuisance.' She looked up at us. 'Someone was supposed to pick me up.'

'Where do you need to go?' I asked.

'The Edgecumbe Arms pub at the Cremyll ferry.'

'My uncle Bill runs the local cab company,' I said. 'He could take you. I can call him if you like.'

Mrs Axford smiled. 'Told you Squidge was a useful man to know.'

'Oh, don't worry,' said Charlotte raising an eyebrow again. 'I've realised that already.'

I was definitely feeling nervous now. This woman fancies me, I thought. She was giving me another of her probing looks. I got a sudden urge to go cross-eyed or pick my nose. Anything to break the intensity of her gaze. Strangely, Lia didn't seem phased at all by this woman staring at me. Neither did her mum, in fact she had this weird smirk on her face.

'Charlotte,' said Mrs Axford, 'don't you think you ought to tell Squidge who you are?'

Lia nodded.

'I guess,' she said, grinning. Then she turned to me. 'I should have said, really. I'm Charlotte Bennett . . .'

I nodded politely. Was I suppose to know the name? Clearly the answer was 'yes'. Maybe she'd been some really famous model on the pages of *Vogue* in the sixties? I mentally scanned pages I'd seen in photography books. Chrissie Shrimpton. Marie Helvin. Jerry Hall. Nope, Charlotte Bennett wasn't ringing a bell. Charlotte Bennett. Charlotte Bennett . . .

It took a moment for the penny to drop, then I slapped my forehead. 'As in Charlie! Oh, peanuts. I thought he, you, were a man!'

Charlotte smiled. 'Most people do,' she said. 'And seeing as I'm coming clean here, I think it's also only fair to tell you that the guy doing the hiring – he's my nephew Roland.'

Great galloping gonadias, I thought, as my whole conversation with her played back through my head at high speed. I'd insulted her nephew, called him a prat, and carried on about movies as though she was an outsider, when, all the time, she was Charlie Bennett, the director of the film. 'Major major bumroll,' I said. 'Didn't realise. Excuse me while I go outside, dig a hole and bury myself in it.'

But Charlotte was laughing. 'No need for that,' she said. 'In fact, one of the things I have to do this afternoon is check locations. So . . . I was wondering, if it wasn't too much trouble, could you get me that cab and maybe come with me and show me that ruin at Penlee Point?'

'Me? Really? Yeah, you betcha.' I quickly pulled out my mobile and dialled my uncle's taxi firm.

On the way out to Penlee Point, we drove down through Kingsand village. As we passed the pub at the bottom of the hill, I spotted Roland sitting on a bench outside. He had a beer in his hand and was talking into his mobile.

Charlotte rolled her eyes as we drove past. 'He's supposed to be my personal assistant as well as third production assistant, which between you and me means 'general dogsbody with a posh title'. One of his jobs is to ferry me about but I can never get through to him – he's always on his phone! So, lesson number one on a film set, Squidge: if you're on a personal call, for whatever reason, keep it short. Better still, don't take or make them when you're on duty. And *always* keep your phone switched on if you're a runner. I'm forever getting Roland's answering service.'

'You just give me a call if ever you get stuck, love,' said Uncle Bill, from the front. He glanced at me in the rear-view mirror and winked. I gave him a huge smile back. Like the rest of the village, he wanted to be part of the production.

'Don't worry, Bill. I've already put your company's number into my phone,' said Charlotte. 'It's always good to have back-up.'

After that, she didn't speak for a while. She was obviously taking in the landscape as we wound our way along the main street, round the top of the village and out through the wood towards Penlee Point. I knew not to disturb her thoughts. She'd be seeing things in her mind as though through the camera's eye, imagining which backdrop would work in which scene and which wouldn't. As we reached the end of the wood, the road became a track then opened out into a clearing. Bill parked the car and settled down to read his newspapers. Charlie and I followed the rest of the path until it led up on to a grassed area and meandered off to the right.

'Wow,' said Charlotte, as she took in the view that suddenly opened up to us. 'This is beautiful.'

There was sea as far as the eye could see. On the left was the cove of Cawsand with the coast beyond stretching out to Mount Edgecumbe then, in the distance, you could see Plymouth. On the right, the landscape was untamed. Fields of grass along the cliff face stretching out for miles to where Rame Head jutted out into the sea.

Charlotte, or as she now insisted I call her, Charlie, looked well impressed. She looked around, at the rocks, at the wind-torn landscape and nodded her head.

I led her out towards the edge of the cliff.

'Absolutely perfect,' she said. 'This place will be great.'

'Ah, but there's more,' I said. 'We're actually standing on the roof of the ruin, though you'd never know it.' I led her down a narrow path on the cliffside a little way to the left. There, concealed below the grassy knoll, was a hiding place in the cliff face. Carved out of stone, it was a cave in the rocks and made the perfect shelter.

'Magwich's hang out, don't you think?' I asked.

'Definitely,' said Charlie. Chuckling, she pointed to the charred remains of a fire and a couple of empty lager cans in the corner. 'In fact, it looks like he's been here already.'

We sat in the ruin and gazed out at the scene for a while then Charlie took some photos and notes. I wish I could see inside her head, I thought enviously. I bet she's working out what angle to shoot from, what time of day to film, where to do close ups, where to film wide angles.

When she was finished, she looked well pleased.

'Back to Cremyll, miss?' asked Uncle Bill, when we got back to the car.

She nodded. 'But can we pass through Kingsand again?'

'Anywhere you like,' said Bill.

She's going to pick up her nephew, I thought. I was still feeling bad about having slagged him off so I decided that when we got into the car, I'd say something to apologise.

'I really am sorry about, you know, before,' I said, as

Uncle Bill drove us through the wood and back towards the village. 'I didn't realise Roland was your nephew.'

Charlotte smiled. 'He's my step-sister Janie's son. Only child, may I add. We've never been close as I've been in the States for years. I'm only just getting to know him. When Janie heard that I would be over doing this film, she asked if I'd give him a job. He finished his degree in media studies last summer so this gives him a chance to see if he wants to work in this area of the industry. You don't know until you've worked on a real film set what it's like and it can come as a shock to some people. It's much harder than you imagine. But he's been doing a good job so far.' Then she grinned. 'Apart from not ever answering his phone. But I believe in giving people a chance. How else is anybody ever going to learn?'

'I really am sorry . . . I didn't know . . .'

She smiled. 'Hey, no worries. He may be my nephew but that doesn't mean I don't know that he can be a bit of a tosser on occasion. But, as I said, he'll learn.'

I almost choked laughing as the car approached the pub where we'd seen Roland earlier.

'Er, Bill, could you slow down a moment,' said Charlie, as we spotted Roland. He was still at the same table and still had his mobile stuck to his ear. She rolled down her window as Bill slowed the car down.

'Hey, Roland,' she called. 'Try and keep the phone line free in working hours. Oh, and this is Squidge. I just hired him so make sure you put his name on the books.'

She rolled her window back up and the car picked up speed. I turned round to look out of the back window. Roland was gawking after us with his jaw hanging open.

5

No Business Like Show Business

THE FOLLOWING Monday, Mac and I set out for our first experience of the wonderful world of film. I felt fantastic. T.T.T. Tip Top Tastic. This was my dream and it was about to come true. I'd be working in the movies and mixing with the stars.

We'd heard that Savannah, the American teen star, was going to be playing the part of Estella as a young woman, and Donny Abreck was taking time out from his band's European tour to play Pip. Mac was over the moon as Savannah was one of his pin ups. At least she used to be before he removed all his babe posters so that Becca wouldn't get jealous when she came back to his bedroom. I couldn't wait. I'd be rubbing shoulders with celebs. I'd be a part of it. *Nothing* could be more glamorous. I felt like this was the beginning of the rest of my life.

We'd been told to report to the unit base that had been set up in the car park to the right of the main house on the Mount Edgecumbe estate.

'Get a load of this!' gasped Mac as we rode up the drive on our trusty bikes and got our first glimpse of the set.

'Looks like the circus has come to town,' I said, parking my bike and taking in all the trailers, vans and cars that had taken over the car park in the last few days. The set was far bigger than anything I'd imagined and already was humming with activity. People were buzzing around looking purposeful and important. There were workmen carrying ladders, cables and tool kits; others were erecting a marquee at the back of the car park; others were putting up what looked like outside loos. Girls in parkas were rushing about, shouting into mobiles; others – the actors, I supposed – looking more relaxed, lounging about in the catering tent, drinking tea and reading their scripts.

Some bloke in a black puffa jacket pointed out the production office, which I'd been told to ask for, and Mac took off towards the back of the car park to begin his car-washing service under the watchful eye of the security men. As I set off to find Roland, I saw Cat waving at me from a marquee with a trailer behind it over in the right-hand corner of the car park. No harm in just saying hi, I thought, as the inviting aroma of bacon and toast wafted my way.

'Posh nosh,' she said, pointing to tables heaving with serving dishes. 'Eggs, bacon, croissants, coffee, fruit – you name it, it's here. Becca and I haven't drawn breath since we started. It was only an hour ago but I feel like I've done a full day's work already. Everyone's been stuffing their faces non stop.'

'An army marches on its stomach,' I said. 'So give us a bacon sarnie.'

'Coming up,' said Cat, reaching for the bacon.

Just as I was taking my first bite, I felt a hand on my shoulder.

'Skiving already?' said Roland.

'Nuuoo,' I protested through a mouth of bacon.

He looked at his watch. 'Four minutes past eight. You were supposed to be here at eight.'

'I was,' I said. 'Sorry. I was just on my way.'

Roland glanced at the sandwich in my hand. 'Yeah, I can see that.'

Cat gave me a sympathetic look behind his back before turning away and beginning to load bread into a toaster.

'Right,' said Roland. 'First job. Some of the actors are on health kicks and no way would they eat any of this.' He indicated the food in the tent. 'They only eat organic. So, Squidge, I trust that you do *do* organic down here in the country?'

'Yeah, think so,' I said. Like, yeah, course, I wanted to

say. Where does he think he is? Clearly to him, this is the back of the back of beyond and it's a surprise that we have electricity. Organic wouldn't be a problem. Cat's dad runs the local store, and he does the full range, some of it supplied by Becca's dad, fresh from his allotment. But I decided not to be a know it all. I needed to get on with Roland so I wanted him to feel like he had the upper hand.

'Think so, won't do,' said Roland. 'Know so. We need food that hasn't been sprayed with chemicals and doesn't contain preservatives or additives. Savannah, for one, won't eat anything else when she gets here. And she only eats wheat-free bread; apparently she's glucose intolerant. So, here's a list. I expect you'll have to go across to Plymouth,' he said smirking, 'or even Exeter, so I'll give you until lunch-time.'

Easy peasy, I thought. It would take me ten minutes to get to Cat's dad's shop. Ten minutes there and ten minutes back. But I wasn't going to let Roland know that. He obviously thought he'd set me a horrible task that was going to take me hours. I didn't feel it was my place to disillusion him.

As I walked to my bike, I realised that he hadn't given me the list, so I backtracked and found him in the production office. He was in there with a couple of the girls I'd seen earlier.

He smirked when he saw me, and held up the list. 'Forget this, did you?'

'Actually *you* forgot to give it to me,' I said, before I could stop myself. 'And I need some cash to pay for it all.'

He gave me a pitying look, counted out some notes, then glanced at one of the girls, as if to say, 'What can you do with these country idiots?'

I stepped up and took the list. 'Thank you so much, sir.'

One of the girls laughed and Roland looked perplexed for a moment like he wasn't quite sure what was going on.

Eejit, I thought as I left.

Roland had me go back and forth between the village and unit base time after time, all day. This actor wanted spring water, and only Evian mind you, nothing else would do. Another actor wanted gingko biloba capsules, to help their memory, another wanted postcards, another fags, another stamps. Then one wanted Earl Grey tea but when I turned up with it, Roland told me it had to be decaffeinated. When I came back with the decaffeinated tea I was told another actor wanted green tea. This was when I began to realise that Roland was taking the piss. He could have got himself organised and given me one long shopping list, so that I could have bought everything in one trip. But then, that would have taken the fun out of it for him. Clearly, giving me a hard time was one of the perks of his job. What's that quote? I asked myself. Mine is not to question why; mine is just to do or die. That's it. Or is until I am a director with my own team of runners. The likes of Roland won't even get a look in on my film sets.

At around five o'clock, I was returning from yet another trip, when I saw a familiar figure striding across the grass towards one of the actors' trailers. It was Martin Bradshawe. *The* Martin Bradshawe. Actor, pianist and legend in his own time though he was a pianist before he really became famous, and a lot of people who know his face from TV or movies don't know about that part of his career. What was he doing here? Which part was he playing? Before I knew it, I'd shot across and was walking next to him.

'Hi, I'm a runner. Can I get you anything?' I asked.

Martin turned and smiled. 'A decent coffee and a packet of fags wouldn't go amiss,' he said. Then he jerked his finger towards the catering trailer. 'The machine in there's *kaput* and they can only do instant. Sorry, but I don't do instant. I think it's sacrilege against the great God of Coffee Beans.'

'Filter or espresso?'

'Oh, don't tease me.'

'I'm not.'

'Espresso.'

'Back in a minute,' I said.

I ran to my bike and rode like the wind until I reached the pub by the ferry. I flew through the door. There was my cousin Arthur behind the bar, as always.

'All right, Arthur?'

Arthur grunted. He was never one for conversation, but he did like his coffee. He owned a cappuccino machine, a filter machine, a cafetiere and numerous other coffee-making appliances. He'd got married only the year before and for a laugh, lots of the family got him coffee makers as wedding presents. 'Makes a change from toasters,' my Uncle Bill had said. Now Arthur has the best collection of coffee machines in the south west. Within minutes, I had hot, fresh coffee in a flask and was racing back to the actors' trailer with it.

Martin couldn't believe it. Nor could he believe I knew about his career as a musician.

'You're kidding,' I said. 'My dad's got all your CDs. I grew up with your music.'

After that there was no stopping us. I found out that he was playing the part of Mr Jaggers, the lawyer, and we got talking about music, movies and coffee. We were getting along like a house on fire, discussing our favourite movies (*Citizen Kane* directed by Orson Welles for him and *Reservoir Dogs* directed by Quentin Tarantino for me), when suddenly a dark shape appeared at the trailer door. It was Roland.

'Ah, Squidge. Where have you been?'

'Um, getting coffee for Mr Bradshawe,' I blustered. I hadn't stopped for a break all day so I figured it would be all right to chat to Martin for just a few minutes.

'And what are you doing in here?'

'Um, talking to Mr Bradshawe.'

'Word in private,' said Roland. Giving me a really false smile as he beckoned me out.

I followed him and as soon as we were out of hearing distance, he turned to me with a face like thunder.

'What the *hell* were you doing in there?'

'Just chatting,' I said. 'I couldn't believe it. Martin Bradshawe. He's a legend.'

Roland obviously didn't share my enthusiasm. 'Legend or not, you keep out of the actors' trailers. The actors aren't interested in the likes of you. Don't try to get friendly with them. They don't want it. You have to know your place on a set like this. There are the stars and there are the runners and the two don't mix.'

'We were getting on great.'

'He was being polite.'

'I was trying to make him feel comfortable.'

'Not your job, mate.'

Part of me wanted to say, 'I'm not your mate, mate' but

I bit my tongue. It was only my first day and I didn't want to blow it with him. Like it or not, he was the one I took my orders from and I had to play the game.

I glanced at my watch. Only half an hour to go before the end of the day. 'So what would you like me to do next?' I asked.

Roland grinned. 'Savannah will be here at the end of the week. So her trailer needs a bit of cleaning, nothing too bad.'

No problem, I thought. Cleaning I can do. I've always done my share of chores at home. Mum says she doesn't want her kids going out into the big, wide world without a clue about how to look after themselves.

'Over here,' said Roland, pointing to a large trailer to the left of the car park.

As he started off towards the trailer, I saluted behind his back and fell into step, marching behind him like he was an army major and I was a soldier. Martin Bradshawe came out and stood on the steps of his trailer. I could see he was laughing.

'She has her own private facilities,' explained Roland as he led me up into an enormous Winnebago. It was fabulous inside. Like one of those rooms you see on decorating programmes on the telly after the experts have been in: simple, tasteful, all soft colours, minimalist furniture.

'Looks immaculate to me,' I said.

'Yeah, should be,' said Roland. 'The cleaners have been in all day, but they've just knocked off and didn't get this bit cleaned . . .' He opened a door to the right of the trailer. 'Smells like some real yob was in here.'

He didn't need to tell me more. The stench finished the story. Disgusting and a half. No way could a babe like Savannah use it. She'd probably sue.

'It's been left locked up and it obviously wasn't cleaned after it was last used,' said Roland. 'It needs airing, scrubbing, disinfecting – I want it smelling of roses by the time you've finished.'

With that, he left, but not before giving me a big, cheesy grin. He was enjoying every second. I looked back at the stinky room. I was supposed to finish at six but this was a job that would take ages.

I set off for the cleaning trailer and bumped into Mac, who was just getting ready to leave for the day. He held up his hands. 'If I have to do any more washing, I think I may lose the will to live,' he said.

'Tough day?' I asked.

Mac nodded then shrugged and shook his head. 'Yeah, actually, no. It's been OK. There are some nice people around here and we've had a laugh. It's just that washing cars gets tedious after the first few. Meeting some of the make-up girls made up for it though. Have you checked them out yet?'

I shook my head.

'Some hot babes. Like the girls you get on make-up counters in big department stores. They're a breed all of their own. One of them, Julie, keeps checking I've had a break and a hot drink and so on. I think she wants to take me home and mother me.'

'Better not let Becca catch you,' I said.

'I know,' said Mac. 'She's been watching me like a hawk. But no worries, it's only a bit of fun. Julie's probably twice my age. So how's your day been?'

I filled him in on the trips back and forth to the village and told him about the last job Roland had given me.

'Oh, tough call,' he sympathised. 'Here, I'll help you get some stuff together.'

We gathered up some cleaning things from the supplies cupboard, then, with rubber gloves and bucket in hand, we walked over to Savannah's Winnebago. As soon as I opened the door to the bathroom, Mac held his nose.

'Woah, Major Stinkingtons, sir,' he grimaced. 'Who's been in this trailer before it came here? A bunch of football yobs with a taste for curried eggs and pickle?'

'By the smell, something like that, I reckon,' I said. 'Anyway, thanks for the cleaning stuff. I guess you'll be off now.'

Mac looked at his watch. 'Yeah, my shift has finished for the day.' He surveyed the room. 'This is going to take you ages.'

I nodded. 'Tell me about it. Best get started . . .'

Mac let out a huge sigh. 'Peanuts. I can't leave you with this. I'll give you a hand. Many hands make light work, etc, etc.'

I could have hugged him. 'You're a real mate,' I said. 'I owe you one.'

And so ended my first day: on my hands and knees with my face down a very pongy loo.

'Welcome to the glamorous world of the movies,' laughed Mac, as he dowsed the toilet bowl with pine disinfectant.

'Yeah right,' I said as I got down on my knees and wiped some suspicous slimy soap remains from the bottom of the shower unit. 'Eukkkk.'

Mac grinned. 'OK, time for a tune. Ready . . . And a one, a two, a one two three . . .'

'There's no business like show business,' we sang, as we tried to ignore the smell and scrubbed.

6 Starstruck

FOR THE first week, I cleaned, I fetched, I carried. I fell into bed at night then dragged myself out of it early each morning. At unit base, Roland clearly had it in for me, and there was nothing I could do to win him over. Charlie gave me a wave sometimes when she saw me and once even came over and asked how I was getting on. 'Great,' I said. I wasn't going to tell tales on Roland the Rat. I've had to deal with boys like him all my life. There's one in every year at school, so he was nothing new.

By the end of the week I was shattered. It was hard work, and a few fellow workers from our school quit. But for me that wasn't an option: I still had my camcorder to replace or repair. And despite the hard work, for the most part, I was enjoying myself immensely and wouldn't have missed the experience for the world.

On Saturday morning, I rolled out of bed extra early. It was the big day: Savannah was due to arrive that morning and I wanted to be sure that I made a good impression. Although there were a few big names in the production, she would be my first encounter with a real superstar. Savannah and Donny Abreck were the only two who were mega, as in known all over the world. It was awesome that I would be on the same set as them.

As I fumbled my way into the bathroom and reached into my soap bag for my razor, my thoughts turned to Lia. I'd managed to put my big foot in it with her yesterday. She'd phoned to tell me that Charlie had asked if she'd like to be an extra in the ballroom scene that they were filming tonight.

'*You?*' I'd said. I guess I must have sounded incredulous, as she was quiet for a few moments.

'Yeah, me,' she'd said finally. 'Why not?'

'Loads of reasons,' I'd said. 'Charlie must be mad. I would never cast you as an extra . . .'

She'd hung up on me before I could explain that an extra has to be in the background and a girl as beautiful as her would attract attention away from the main action. She'd left her phone on answer all evening. I'd left loads of messages asking her to call me back but she hadn't.

Must get things sorted with her, I thought, as I looked for Dad's shaving foam. Time for my fortnightly shave! It's a weird thing, shaving, I thought as I frothed up my face. I looked forward to having enough facial hair to shave for ages, thinking that when it finally happened I'd turn into a grown up overnight. But now I've started having to shave regularly, I can tell already it's going to be a nuisance. It takes ages and you have to be really careful that you don't nick yourself, as even though there are self-protector blades, they don't allow for the occasional teenage zit. Whack the top off one of those and it's ER central.

Girls think they have it bad with periods and stuff, but that's just once a month. A bloke has to shave every day. Well, in the end you do; it's only once every two weeks for me at the moment, but even that is boring. Why can't you just shave once and that's it? I mean, where does all the hair keep coming from? Cat used to have this doll when she was little that had all its hair coiled up inside its head, and you could pull it out or push it back so the doll had either a long or a short hairstyle. When I was a kid, I used to think that it was the same for humans. We all had an allotted amount of hair stuffed in our bodies, all coiled around and around like in the doll, and it grew out until there was none left and that's when people went bald. Hair – where does it come from? I wondered, as I carefully shaved the fuzz off my chin. Not much there, really, but enough to look a bit naff if it's left.

I was hoping I'd get a hairy chest, but I don't think it's going to happen. So far, I have four hairs: three on one side of my left nipple and one on the right. Elsewhere is all as per normal though, armpits, legs, pubes. Mac knows this interesting thing to do with pubes. A mate of his from London had shown him. (He lived there, before his parents got divorced.) You pull out a few of your pubic hairs and put them in an ashtray or something. Then you light them with a match. It's amazing: they dance. Seriously – dance. It's a real laugh. Course, after Mac had shown me, we wanted to show Cat, Becca and Lia and see if girl's pubes did the same. But they came over all coy and prissy and said it wasn't ladylike. Girls aren't really impressed by stuff like that.

They didn't want to see Mac light his farts, either. He's a total master at it and it could have been his party piece except only the boys wanted to watch, while the girls went all girlie and pulled disgusted faces. They don't kid me; I know girls fart too, only I guess they call it breaking wind in the same way that where boys sweat, girls are only meant to glow. What rubbish. We all have bodies and bodily functions, and sometimes you have to let one go. Mac takes it a bit far sometimes, though. He wafts his towards you, then comments on it as though it was a really fine wine. 'Ummm, get this one,' he'll say proudly. 'Rich and hearty, with just a hint of broccoli.' He can empty a room if he wants to with some of his S.B.Ds. (Silent but deadlies.) Sometimes the girls don't like it when we act too laddish in front of them, like it turns them off, so now I'm careful to keep stuff like that to when Mac and I are on our own.

My mental meandering on the subject of pubes and farting was interrupted, as my eye fell upon the toothpaste and I remembered something that Mac had told me to try with it, when I dropped him off at his house last night. I glanced at my watch. I had a few minutes to spare. I could try it. It was something that he'd read in a mag. One of those mags he's not to supposed to have, I may add. One of those mags you find on the top shelf in newsagents, and under the mattress at Mac's.

'The mag said that if you put toothpaste on your willie, it makes it bigger,' he said.

'Never,' I said.

'For real,' he said. 'Something to do with the menthol having a stimulating effect, so blood rushes to cool your willie and it grows. Something like that. Sounded very scientific.'

Course I stored that bit of info away immediately, as willie size is one of my private concerns. I mean, how are you supposed to know what's big, small or average? I guess it's a bit like girls worrying about the size of their bum or the size of their boobs. A boy's hang up is how does he score in the trouser-snake department.

Well, let's see if it works, I thought, as I took the top off the tube, and applied the toothpaste liberally.

About twenty seconds later, the menthol kicked in.

'ARGhhhhhhhhhhhhhhhhhhhhhhhhhhhhhhhhhhhhhhhhhhh! Oo, oo, ahoo, aah, aah, arghhhhhhhhhhhhhhhhhhhhhhhhhhhh hhh!'

My eyes began to stream, my breath shortened and my willie stang like someone had put it in a mincer. Talk about stimulant effect! I was going to go through the roof. What to do? What to do? Somewhere in the recesses of my brain I remembered something from a first-aid course I did years ago, something about milk being a good neutraliser, with soothing properties. If nothing else, it would certainly be cold. Got to get downstairs, I told myself. Why did I try it? I must be stupid. Big mistake, big mistake, I thought, as I hopped downstairs. Remind me to kill Mac when I see him, that's if I don't die first. I can see the headlines now: *'Teenage todger totalled in toothpaste terror!'* On my grave, they'll write, 'He died young but his nether regions were minty fresh.' Oh, *argghhhhhhhhh*. Maybe I picked the wrong brand, or something. Oo, ar, the *pain*! I thought I was going to pass out with it.

I reached the kitchen. Luckily there was no one around. I flung the fridge door open. Milk. Where was it? Murphy's

Law: only a thimbleful left and the milkman wasn't due for another half hour. What else? Need something cold, something to cool it down. I scanned the contents of the fridge. Carton of minestrone soup? I don't *think* so. Vegetables? No. Ham? Cheese? The stinging sensation was getting worse. 'Quick, Squidge, *do* something,' cried my poor willie. Yoghurt! There was a pot of it at the back on the top shelf. Strawberry flavoured. That will do, I thought, as I quickly grabbed the pot, pulled off the lid and plunged my willie into the cool, soft liquid. 'Ahhhh,' I sighed, as the stinging sensation began to ease.

Unfortunately, just at that moment, Dad came through the back door. Try explaining your way out of this one! I thought, as he stopped mid-whistle and looked at me quizzically. I had to make something up, but what? How do you explain? Like, oh yeah, just trying the toothpaste on the old fella trick. You know how it is, Dad?

Instead I grinned sheepishly and said, 'Strawberry yoghurt – just can't get enough of it.'

Dad gave me a strange look. 'Your willie isn't a straw, son,' he said. He shook his head as if he didn't quite believe what he was seeing, then sighed and muttered something about adolescence, before going upstairs.

Thank goodness the yoghurt had done the trick. Had I done something wrong? I wondered, as I followed Dad up a few minutes later. Maybe you have to use the toothpaste brands with flouride. I passed Dad on the stairs, this time he was coming down.

'You all right?' he asked looking at me with concern.

'I'm fine,' I mumbled.

I don't know why he's worried. I'm not the only one in this family obsessed by my willie. I remember when Will was about three years old, Mum found him in the garden rubbing the end of his with a toothbrush. When she asked what he was doing, he said, 'I'm cleaning its teeth.' We all thought it was so cute. But even at that age, he saw his willie as having a separate identity. Girls are so lucky they don't have them.

Once I was shaved and showered, I nicked a bit of Dad's Armani aftershave then went to dress: white T-shirt, Levi jeans, Converse All Stars sneakers. My James Dean, Rebel-without-a-Cause look, completed with the all important leather jacket and dark shades. Bit of gel to get my hair spiked up, and I was ready to roll.

Next on the agenda was to pick up Mac. Like me, he smelt of expensive aftershave. I guess he was looking forward to meeting Savannah as well. 'Chanel for Men?' I asked.

'Mum got it me for Christmas,' he said, then sniffed my neck. 'Armani?'

'Only the best,' I said, as we set off on our bikes. 'Um, tried the toothpaste thing. Don't recommend it.'

Mac laughed. 'Me, too. I mean me neither. Only I couldn't find the toothpaste, so I thought I'd try something else with a menthol ingredient – Deep Heat. I almost passed out.'

'Tell me about it,' I said, then told him about my conversation with Lia.

'And now she's giving you the silent treatment?' he asked.

I nodded. 'I'm going to ask Cat to talk to her for me,' I called over my shoulder.

As soon as we reached the set, I went to the catering tent to find Cat and asked if she would try and get through to Lia for me.

'You don't know a lot about girls do you,' she said, after I'd filled her in on Lia's reaction.

'What do you mean?'

'Lia probably thought you meant that you wouldn't cast her because she'd be no good.'

'But she should know me better than that,' I said. 'Of course that's not what I meant.'

'So why wouldn't you have cast her as an extra?' she asked, pouring tea out of a huge tea pot.

'Extras are supposed to be in the background, to blend

into a crowd,' I explained. 'No one should draw the audience's attention away from the main performers, from what's happening centre stage. Put a girl as stunning as Lia in the background and what do you have? Major distraction. So they're making a big mistake in my book.'

'Oh, I see,' said Cat. 'Hey, that's really sweet. Why didn't you tell her that?'

'Because, being stupid, it came out all wrong. Or at least, it didn't come out at all. Sometimes I forget that people can't read my thoughts. So, will you tell her for me?'

'Sure.'

Most of the day was taken up with dressing the set for the ballroom scene, and I didn't see much of anybody. Everywhere there was a blur of activity with people racing to get everything done on time. Course, Roland had to have his say about not bugging Savannah when she arrived. Mid-afternoon, he gathered the team of runners around him.

'Savannah doesn't like to mix with the rest of the crew, so we have to respect her need for privacy as an artist. Get that, Squidge?' he said, looking pointedly at me. 'You in particular. I know how starstruck you can be and I don't want you acting like a country bumpkin who has never seen a celebrity.'

As if, I thought. I'm way cooler than that. Why did he

have to come out with stuff like that in front of other people? It made me look a right prat. But then, I guess that's exactly what he intended.

'Shan't even look at her, sir,' I said. 'I'll keep my eyes down, might doff my cap, that's all, sir.'

Roland gave me a filthy look then started handing out the next lot of assignments. Mine was to take the costume that Savannah would be wearing up to the main house, so that she could change up there later on that evening. It was a stunning dress, all lace and tiny pearl buttons. The genuine article, borrowed from a museum up in London.

I hadn't had anything to eat since breakfast, and when I got back to unit base after delivering the dress, I was totally starving. I looked in quickly at the catering tent and, as lunch was long over, one of the girls there piled my plate up with what was left – doughnuts. They had some fab looking ones, fresh, sugary and oozing jam. I ate one and stuffed a couple into my pockets to eat later.

I decided to take one over to Mac, as I know he loves doughnuts. Just as I was crossing the centre of the camp, I saw Lia chatting to Cat and Becca outside the loos. Cat gave me the thumbs up, indicating that she had explained to Lia what I really meant by not casting her as an extra. Lia looked up and smiled, and I felt my heart start to thump in my chest, like it always did when I saw her. Back on track,

I thought. It felt great and I wanted her to know how happy I felt. Only one thing a boy can do in a situation like that to show how he feels, and that is to demonstrate his range of Silly Walks *à la* John Cleese in *Monty Python*. I pushed my chest out, made myself go knocked kneed and started jerking my head backwards and forwards like a pigeon, as I took a few steps. The girls cracked up. Sufficiently encouraged, I went into my impersonation of an Egyptian dancer doing the sand dance.

Suddenly I saw Becca's face register surprise. She pointed towards Savannah's trailer and started waving her arms at me to stop. 'Ohmigod, I didn't know she'd arrived,' I heard her say.

I turned to where she was looking. There was a pretty redhead at the window of the Winnebago. Not just any old pretty redhead. It was the one and only *Savannah*. She'd been watching me loon about, and was laughing. My knees turned to jelly then my legs turned to rubber. I didn't know whether to go backwards, forwards or sideways. I was so embarrassed that she'd been watching me, was *still* watching me. I gave her a half wave and moved forward. While I was looking at Savannah, I didn't notice a roll of cable in front of me and I tripped and fell flat on my face. Hmm, that's one way to make a good first impression, I thought, as jam from the doughnuts in my pockets went squirting everywhere.

I rolled over onto my back and started to sit up. Next thing I knew, Savannah had opened her trailer door, run over to me, knelt beside me and was peering anxiously at me.

'Are you all right?' she cried. 'You're bleeding.' She looked around but the girls made themselves scarce and there was only Roland who had just appeared from the production trailer.

'Is there a medical trailer?' asked Savannah. 'Someone who can help? Please, someone, *do* something!'

Roland stood over us, looking bemused.

She leaned over me again and looked into my eyes. 'Just lie still. We'll get help.'

Although it was very tempting to lie there and act dumb, I thought I'd better come clean. But then Roland would be mad. Maybe I should stay quiet. Oh God, I thought, as I remembered Roland's earlier lecture about not even looking at Savannah. Now here I was with my head in her lap, my nose almost in her very famous chestie bits. Not quite the dignified first meeting I'd imagined.

'Er, jam,' I admitted. 'It's jam, not blood. Sorry, sorry. Raspberry to be precise. Doughnuts.' And I sat up and showed her the squashed cakes.

Her eyes widened. 'Doughnuts?'

I nodded, wondering if she was going to get mad and get

me the sack. Roland had said that she didn't like to mix with the crew at all. But no, she was leaning towards me and whispering in my ear in her cute Texan drawl.

'Can you get me some? I *love* doughnuts, but my stupid minders only ever let me have health food.'

I smiled up at her. 'Consider it done.'

She got up. 'What's your name?'

'Squidge.'

She laughed. 'Kind of what you did to the doughnuts, eh? Anyway, my trailer in five minutes.' Then she looked at Roland. 'And you are?'

'Um, third production assistant,' he said, with what I think was supposed to be a winning smile. 'Call me Roland.'

She turned her back on him. 'Whatever.' And with a conspiratorial wink at me, she sashayed off.

'*YEEESSSSS*,' said a triumphant voice in my head.

7 Disaster

IN THE DAYS after her arrival, Savannah seemed to adopt me as her personal runner, calling me into her trailer first thing and sending for me throughout the day. She was the only one of the cast to have asked for my private mobile number, and once she had it, boy, did she use it. 'Squidge, honey . . . do y'all know anywhere I could get . . .' The requests were endless. Roland wasn't very happy about it, but there wasn't a lot he could do; she was the star, not him. And she was amazing. A real celeb. It was an honour to run her errands.

'She ought to have a T-shirt done, saying, "Have entourage, will travel",' joked Mac, when he realised how many people she had with her. There was Hank and Mitch, the security men; Marie Anne, the private masseur who doubled as a yoga teacher; Jons, the stylist; the hairdresser, Chantelle, and the chef called Tone.

Some of the things she asked me to do were bonkers. Like I had to go and buy her Smarties then take out all the red ones because she didn't like red. Mac said to suck the red off and put them back, but I saved them up and gave them to Lia instead; she likes Smarties too. All the gorgeous yellow roses that had been put in her trailer had to be removed and I had to zoom about trying to find white ones, as she only ever had white flowers, preferably white lilies. Then I had to go over to Plymouth to find a particular brand of toothpaste, one that had no mint or menthol in it, because she was taking homeopathic remedies and the mint interfered with them (amongst other things, I thought, as I remembered my own tingly fresh experience). Then I had to go back to Plymouth again to find a particular brand of loo paper. On every trip, my mobile would ring and she'd whisper down the phone a request for some kind of treat to be sneaked in – like a Hershey bar. Then she'd feel guilty that she'd strayed from her organic diet and I'd have to go and get a special brand of spring water, which luckily Cat's dad had in his store. He'd got it in after the local paper printed an article about all the chemicals that are in our water system, and everyone went mad buying bottled water.

'So now you're her private slave?' asked Lia when I returned to unit base with yet another bag of shopping for Savannah.

'Looks like it.' I grinned. 'Why? Are you jealous?'

Lia's face clouded for a moment. 'Do I need to be?'

'No way,' I said and put my arm round her. 'Hey, you know I only have eyes for you.' At this, I pulled out a pair of glass eyes that I'd bought in a joke shop next to the health shop in Plymouth the day before. A boy can never have enough practical jokes ready to play on people, I reckon. My family collects them. So far we have the plastic boobs, a false hand (good for shaking hands with people and letting it come off), a false arm (good for putting next to a tyre so it looks like someone is squashed underneath) and a collection of assorted wigs.

Lia couldn't help laughing. 'You're mad you are,' she said. 'But be serious for a moment. Remember the promise we made to each other on your birthday – to tell each other the truth. That includes telling each other if we fancy anyone else.'

'I fancy you,' I said, dodging the issue. I didn't want to hurt Lia's feelings. Course I fancied Savannah; she's a hot babe and I was in awe of her. But someone as famous as her would never fancy a nobody like me, not in a million years. I'm not in the contest, so why cause trouble?

It was at the end of the second week of filming that things took a turn for the worse between Roland and me. The ballroom scene had gone well, but Charlie wanted to do some retakes of Savannah in the lovely, old dress. Only the dress wasn't so lovely anymore. A rumour had got around that it had a huge stain right down the front of it, and guess who was getting the blame . . . Right – me. But I knew that the last time I'd seen that dress was when I'd dropped it off on Saturday, just before the doughnut incident, and then it was definitely *sans* stain. I think I'd have remembered spilling what they were saying looked like coffee over it. Word got around the base: disaster; Squidge is a clumsy oaf; the museum will sue . . . To make matters worse, it was needed for the shoot that evening to keep Charlie on schedule and within budget. Everything and everybody had been set up for the scene, then Rosie, the costume girl, discovered the dress. She sent for Roland, and Roland sent for me.

I raced over to the production office.

'You total, total idiot,' he yelled.

'But it wasn't me,' I objected. 'Honest. For a start I don't drink coffee.'

'How very convenient,' said Roland, with a look that told me that whatever I said, he wasn't going to believe it.

'No point in crying over spilled whatever,' said Charlie, coming into the trailer behind us. 'Let's get off who is or who isn't to blame. Let's deal with the situation. We have a problem – can we come up with a solution?'

'What time do you need the dress by?' I asked.

'It has to be a night shoot again, so we can start as soon as the light has gone. So about nine, nine fifteen,' she looked at her watch and grimaced. 'It's gone six thirty so the cleaners will be shut by now, and we can't touch a dress like that ourselves or the museum really will sue us. It has to be done by a professional and even then I don't know if the stain can be removed.' Then she looked at us both. 'Mistakes happen. Things get broken; things get split. On a set this big, it's to be expected. What upsets me, though, is that whoever did this, didn't let me know straight away, while the cleaners were still open and something could still be done about it.'

Roland gave me a filthy look. I gave him one back.

'My aunt Bea can fix it,' I said. 'She runs the cleaners over in Torpoint.'

'But will she still be open?' asked Charlie.

I shook my head. 'But she'll open for me.' I said. I felt really bad about the dress. Even though I knew it wasn't me who'd ruined it, I hated to think that Charlie thought I had. 'Don't you worry. I've got friends in high places.'

Charlie smiled back at me. 'If you can sort this, I'll give you your first job when you're out of college.'

I didn't need to hear any more. I rang Uncle Bill who gave me a lift – I didn't want to risk taking the dress on my bike. We drove like the wind to Aunt Bea's. She was a bit put out at first because she was just settling down to watch telly with a cup of tea, but when she heard it was for Savannah, she was pleased to help. Like everyone else in the area, she wanted to have her story to tell about being part of the production. An hour and a half later, we were back on set.

'It's as good as new,' I declared as I handed it over to Rosie. 'Well not new, because it's ancient, but as good as it was before the coffee was spilled over it.'

'You're a star,' she said, as she rushed it over to Savannah's trailer.

On my way home, I got a call from Mac.

'Got some news for you,' he said. 'Jacob, the electrician, told Chantelle from make-up, who told Penny from production, who told Deirdre in the office, who told Josh in the catering tent, and Cat overheard, and she told Becca and she told me . . .'

'Told you what?'

'It was Roland who spilled the coffee. Apparently, Jacob was up at the house fixing the lights for the shoot and he saw Roland go into the dressing room with that skinny, little blond girl, Sandra, the other production assistant from the office, for a snog. They didn't know he could see them and apparently they got a bit carried away and

77

knocked over the coffee, all over the dress. They agreed to hush it up as Sandra was terrified she'd lose her job and Roland, as we know, is a rat.'

'And I was the scapegoat.'

'Exactly.'

'What a creep.'

'Creepiest creep in Creepville,' said Mac.

'I hate that people think it was me, but then I don't want to tell on him. I don't want to be, you know, a sneak . . .'

'You're far too nice, Squidge. But no worries – I'll put it around. And if I don't Chantelle will, so it will get back to Charlie one way or another. You know what those make-up girls are like. If you want to get something round the whole set, just tell one of them and you can guarantee it will be public knowledge in twenty-four hours.'

Phew, I thought, as I turned off my phone after the call. Now I can go home for a bit of a kip without worrying about everything. Bliss. And I had the next day off, too. My first day since I'd started work. I was going to sleep, sleep, sleep, then see Lia in the afternoon. I'd hardly seen Lia since I started work and I was really looking forward to catching up with her properly.

When I woke the next day, the weather was appalling. No matter, I thought, as I turned over to go back to sleep for another hour, I'm as snug as a bug in a rug here. And then my mobile rang.

It was a now-familiar Texan voice. Part of me was thrilled that she'd called me at home. Part of me felt, hey now, time out, this is my day off.

'Hi, Savannah,' I said, wondering what she wanted this time.

'Hey, Squidge. What ya doing?'

'Oh, you know, it's my day off . . .'

'Mine too.'

'I thought you were doing the garden scenes today.'

'Have you looked out of the window?' she asked. 'It's raining. Anyway, Donny's jet-lagged and says he can't possibly be filmed until he's looking his best again.'

'Oh, right,' I said. With the drama of the dress, I'd forgotten the big excitement of yesterday: Donny Abreck had arrived to do his scenes as Pip. 'Shame. Hope it doesn't put Charlie's schedule back.'

'No, she's doing all the interior scenes that she can with Mrs Haversham and Herbert Pocket, so I got me the day off.'

'Great. So what are you going to do?' I asked.

'I want to see Cornwall.'

'Yeah, good idea. It's a fabulous place. Lots to see. Got anywhere in mind?'

'I sure do. I want to see that place where Daphne du

Maurier lived. She's the woman who wrote the novel *Rebecca*. Do you know it?'

'Yeah. She lived down near Fowey. You'll like it there.'

'I was hoping you could take me. Be ma escort.'

Wow, I thought. Me, be her escort. That would be something. But I had neither the transport nor the funds. A celebrity like her probably doesn't carry her own money – like the Queen. And most likely, she'd expect lunch, probably somewhere posh and out of my league. 'I'd love to, Savannah, but my trusty old bike wouldn't last that far. And, let's face it, your minders wouldn't let you out of their sight.'

I heard a long sigh at the other end of the phone. 'That's too bad. I was hoping you might have a car and we could sneak away.'

'Sorry.' I didn't elaborate on why I didn't drive a car. She'd never asked my age and I didn't want to tell her that I was only sixteen, too young to have a licence, in case she thought I was a kid.

When I put the phone down, I felt confused. Should I have fixed it? Got Uncle Bill to drive us? Yes? No? Should I have taken the risk and blown my savings? I didn't know. Spending time away from the set with Savannah, alone with her, would have been a real coup. But then why would she want to spend time with me? I was nobody. Maybe she was bored. Playing with me for a bit of fun? Whatever was going on, I didn't know how to handle it. Course there was a part of me that was flattered, that couldn't wait to tell Mac. But then he'd tell Becca, who'd tell Cat, who'd tell Lia. Plus, another part of me had taken on board what Roland had said: she's the star – don't forget it. I hadn't. I wouldn't. Phew, narrow escape, I thought, as I called Lia and said I'd be up at her house in about an hour.

Just as I was setting off for Lia's, I saw a limo with tinted windows winding its way along the lanes through the village. Might be Donny taking a look round, I thought, as I got out my bike. Then the car turned off into our lane and drove towards our cottage where it slowed down and stopped about a foot away from me. The window of the driver's seat wound down and a chauffeur, complete with cap, looked out at me.

'Are you Mr Squidge?' he asked.

I nodded and tried to peer into the back to see who was in there but I couldn't see anyone.

'Get in,' said the chauffeur.

8

I'm a Celebrity,
Get Me Out of Here

I COULDN'T believe it. Five minutes later, there I was: in the back of a limo with one of the most famous teen stars in the world. Wahey! Me. Squidge. Riding along with Savannah like I was the business. Shame about the tinted windows, I thought, no one could see in and recognise me. Hah, that would have caused a stir in the village. I wanted to wind a window down, stick my head out and yell, 'Yoooohooooo, look where I am! Look who I'm with!'

After the chauffeur had told me to get in, Savannah had leaned forward from the back seat where she was sitting, smiled and said, 'Hey, I'm a celebrity, get me out of here.'

How could I resist? I'll phone Lia as soon as I can, I thought. I'm sure she'll understand. I know I could have refused, could have told Savannah that I had a prior engagement. But, no, I jumped straight in, no questions asked. I did feel a prick of conscience about letting Lia down, but it didn't last long. Things like this don't happen very often, least not to me.

As we drove west, further into Cornwall, I did my best to fill Savannah in on the places of interest along the way. I asked the driver to go via Bodmin Moor so that we could stop at Jamaica Inn for coffee.

'Jamaica Inn has stood high on the moor for over four centuries,' I said, in my best tour-guide voice, repeating what every Cornish schoolboy and girl learns in junior school. 'It is the legendary coaching inn where Daphne du Maurier stayed in 1930. It inspired her to write her novel of the same name, about smuggling and pirates.'

'Wow, this is breathtaking,' said Savannah, taking off her shades and gazing at the bleak, open landscape of the moors that stretched in every direction, as far as the eye could see. 'I'm glad I brought you along, Squidge. We'd never have known about this place without you.'

I didn't tell her that the Inn is featured in every tour book about the area, if she'd only looked. If she wanted to pour praise on me, I wasn't going to stop her.

After coffee at the Inn, we drove down to the seaside resort of Fowey, where we found the Daphne du Maurier Literary Centre. While Savannah was looking at the photos on display, I slipped outside and called Lia's house. Course,

Murphy's Law, the phone was engaged. I called her on her mobile. Her mum answered.

'Hi, Squidge. Lia's gone looking for you. She must have forgotten her mobile as it's here in the hall. Anyway, she thought you must have been called in to work to do more errands . . .'

'Yeah, sort of. So where's she gone looking for me?'

'Down to unit base, I think. Shall I tell her you called?'

'Yeah, thanks, and I'll call her later.'

I glanced in the window at Savannah. She was now busy buying postcards in the gift shop, so I quickly dialled the production office, in the hope that someone other than Roland would pick up.

'Yeah?' droned an unenthusiastic sounding voice.

'Oh, hi Roland, Squidge here.'

'So?'

'Could you . . . er, you know that extra called Lia? The blonde . . .'

'Yeah, fit looking. Course I've noticed her, as in, hubba hubba, who wouldn't? Zac Axford's daughter.'

I didn't know whether to tell him that she was my girlfriend or not. Probably best not as, knowing Roland, he'd make her life miserable just because she was going out with me.

'Could you pass a message on?'

'I think she's out of your league, Squidgola, man,' said Roland.

'Yeah, probably, but could you pass a message on anyway. I was supposed to see her this morning. Could you tell her something came up . . .'

At this point, Roland barked a filthy laugh. 'Yeah right. She has that effect on me too.'

At this point, I decided that it would be stupid to leave a message with Roland. He was totally unreliable and probably wouldn't pass the message on, just to spite me.

'Er, forget it, Roland,' I said. 'I'll sort it.'

Next I called Mac on his mobile. It was switched off, so I began to leave a message on his voicemail. 'Hi, Mac . . .' Then I saw that Savannah was coming out of the centre. I didn't want Mac to hear her voice and suss out that I was with her, then say something that got back to Lia before I had a chance to talk to her myself. I turned away and started gabbling. 'It's really important. Can you tell her, sorry about this afternoon and I'll call her later. If you don't see her, could you ask Becca or Cat to pass on the message – she's bound to stop in to see them. Thanks, mate.'

Now I just have to pray that he picks up his messages, I thought as I clicked the phone shut.

'Who y'all talking to?' asked Savannah.

'Oh, no one,' I said. 'Actually, I was . . .' I decided to

come clean about having a girlfriend. After we'd left Jamaica Inn, Savannah had been very flirty, and although part of me was flattered, there was another part of me that felt panicked. She was a mega-star and if she came on to me, I wouldn't know what to do. We might be acting all 'pals on a day out' today, but I hadn't forgotten that she was one of the biggest stars in the world and though I was doing my best to be cool, inside I felt intimidated. 'I was . . . trying to get in touch with my girlfriend, Lia . . .'

'Oh, her. She's the one with the long, blond hair, isn't she? Someone said she was Zac Axford's daughter.'

I nodded. 'That's right.'

'My mom used to have all his CDs. So she's your girlfriend, huh? Yeah, I have noticed her,' she said. 'Pretty in a kind of obvious way. Course that's not enough to be a star. To be a star, you have to have the X factor.'

'I don't think Lia's bothered about being a star,' I said, smiling. 'Not with most of her family in the public eye in one way or another. You know, dad's a rock star, sister's a model and mum's an ex-model. Lia's different. She's really grounded – it's one of the things I like about her. I reckon she might end up doing something really unshowbusinessy, like being a doctor or a vet.'

'Really?' asked Savannah, then pulled a face. 'A vet? Hmm, don't fancy spending my life with my hand up some cow's ass.' She laughed, but she seemed a bit miffed all the same. Imagine, I thought, Savannah jealous of me having a girlfriend.

The rain clouds from earlier had disappeared, giving way to a perfect, sunny spring day. We had a great time exploring the town. Everywhere we went, heads turned to stare after her. Whether it was because people recognised her or because she looked like she came from a world far away from the Cornish countryside, I don't know.

She was stunning in a Kylie Minogue kind of way and oozed confidence and charisma. She had her chestnut-red hair piled on top of her head and was wearing bright red lipstick, a tiny – and I mean tiny, it barely covered her boobs – one-strap black vest top, a hipster tartan mini-kilt and Doc Marten type lace-up leather boots. With her perfectly-toned stomach on show, complete with pierced belly button, and her amazing long legs, I reckon she'd have stood out in any crowd, especially round here where most people are holiday makers slobbing around in fleeces and tracksuit bottoms.

Men of all ages were almost walking into lamp posts as they turned back to look at her as she cruised by. I felt on top of the world when, at one point, we went to look out at the yachts and passing boats on the estuary, and she took my hand like I was her regular boyfriend.

'Let's pretend we're on holiday here and we're tourists,' she said later, as we browsed in the windows of the antique shop lining the narrow cobblestoned streets that led away from the quay.

'Sure,' I said, with a backwards glance at the chauffeur/body guard. 'Tourists who just happen to be followed by a tough-looking man dressed from head to toe in black. He looks like the bad guy from a Bond movie.'

'Oh, just ignore him,' she said. 'It's in my contract that Mitch goes where I go. Behind the shades, he's a sweetie.'

We walked all over the town, visited Fowey Museum and St Fimbarrus Church, where we signed the guest book, browsed in the shops some more, then stuffed our faces with all the local fare: Cornish pasties, Cornish ice cream, Cox's apple juice from a local orchard. I didn't have to worry once about money because as soon as Savannah saw something she wanted, she gave Mitch a nod and there he was with a wad of cash.

Later we walked along the coast and Savannah took photos outside what's left of St Catherine's Castle. After that, we went back down into the town and took the tourist boat on a short trip up the estuary. It was fabulous looking at the small town from the water and after about ten minutes, we passed the house where Daphne du Maurier had actually lived. 'It's called Ferryside,' I said, as the boat chugged by a lovely old house on the water's edge. 'I think her son lives there now.'

Savannah was thrilled – especially when I told her about the other 'grander' house where Daphne lived later on in her life. 'It's called Menabilly and it's the one she wrote about in her book *Rebecca*, only she changed the name of the house to Manderley for the novel.'

'"Last night I dreamt I went to Manderley again,"' said Savannah, quoting the opening line of the book. 'That's my all-time *favourite* film. It's *sooooo* romantic. It was my grandmother's favourite too. After I'd seen the movie with her, I read all Daphne du Maurier's books, and that's why, when I heard that I was going to be filming down here, I wanted to come and check out where she used to live. But I never dreamed that Manderley was a real place. And still standing. Can we go see it?'

I shook my head. 'It's privately owned and set in it's own grounds. You can't see much from the road.'

'No matter,' she said. 'Let's go when we get off the boat.'

When the boat trip was over, we drove out as close to Menabilly as we could. But, as I'd told her, we couldn't see the house from the road. It didn't dampen Savannah's enthusiasm though. She asked the driver to stop on the road and she photographed the trees outside the estate. 'Even a shot of the trees near Manderley, or Menabilly, or whatever y'all call it, will be awesome,' she said. 'Remember the scene in the film when you see the house for the first time, in the distance, in the mist . . . Fabulous.'

I could have cursed myself for not bringing a camera with me. Me, who travels everywhere with one. The one time I just happen to be hanging out with a superstar, and where is it? In the cupboard at home.

As the day went on, I felt like I got a glimpse of the real girl behind the public image. Beneath the showbiz trimmings, Savannah was an ordinary girl and, I reckon, a bit lonely from being on the road so much. She may be a mega-star, but she's still only seventeen and she misses her home and her family. She treated me like an equal. And I felt I'd made a new friend. She told me all about living in New York and about how she first got started in acting. And I told her all about living in Cornwall and my ambition to be a film director. She was genuinely interested – I could tell. She wasn't just being polite. Someone like her doesn't need to be.

On the way home, she snuggled up against me and fell asleep on my shoulder. For a moment, I let myself imagine what might have happened if I hadn't been going out with Lia and had responded to Savannah's flirtation with a bit more enthusiasm. The thought of it made me shiver inside. If my friends could see me now, I thought, as we hit the A390 and made our way back to the Rame Peninsula and home. The driver dropped me off and I waved as the car drove away.

As soon as I got in, I phoned Lia. It was now six thirty and this time she was at home.

'Hey,' she said.

Amazing, I thought. Girls can say so much in one word. By the flat tone of the 'hey', I could tell she was miffed.

'Sorry about before, Lia. Did Mac give you my message?'

'No, what message? Where have you been?'

'I called Mac's mobile and asked him to tell you I'd call later. Bugger, he can't have picked up his messages. I called unit base to try and reach you, as well, but I got Roland and – '

'Roland? He's here. Hold on, I'll ask him . . .'

'*No*, don't. I didn't leave a message with Roland.'

'But you just said you called him . . .'

This wasn't going well. 'Yes, I *did*. But I didn't leave a message with him. What's he doing there, anyway?'

'He brought us back up to the house. Did you really call? You're not just making it up?'

'*No*, I mean, yes. Yes, I did really call. And no, I'm not making it up. I called this morning to say sorry I couldn't meet you, but your phone was engaged. So then I left a message on Mac's voicemail. Honest. He'll tell you.'

'But why didn't you leave a message when you spoke to Roland?'

'I thought he might not pass it on. You know he's got it in for me.'

'Why? You've never done anything to upset him.'

'Tell *him* that,' I said. 'But he'd probably stir it if he knew we were going out. I know he fancies you.'

I waited for her to say she didn't fancy him but she didn't say anything.

'Anyway, he brought *who* up to your house?' I asked. 'Who's us? Cat and Becca?'

'No, Charlie, Donny and Roland.'

'Donny Abreck?'

'Yeah, he arrived yesterday. Anyway, where have you been?'

'To Fowey.'

'Why?'

'Um, Savannah wanted to go.'

'Ah . . . I thought you might have been with *her*.'

'Yeah, it was good. She's nice. We went to Jamaica Inn, too.'

'You said you'd take me there.'

'I will. Soon, I promise.'

There was a long silence at the other end of the phone.

'You still there, Lia?'

'Yeah.'

Another long silence.

'So, what is it? Are you mad with me? I really did try and phone, you know, and I thought you'd understand . . . And oh, I did speak to your mum. Ask her. She'll tell you that I phoned. On your mobile. You left it behind this morning. Yeah. See, I wouldn't know that if I wasn't telling the truth, would I? Ask your mum.'

'She's gone out to get her hair done.'

'Ask her when she gets back.'

Lia went quiet for a few moments. 'Everyone thinks that you and Savannah fancy each other,' she said, finally.

'No way,' I said. 'Hey come on, Lia . . .'

'Look, got to go,' she said, and I heard voices in the background at Lia's end of the phone. It sounded like a crowd had walked into wherever she was. There was a lot of laughing and loud talking going on. 'We're taking Donny out to dinner. Apparently he doesn't like the hotel where he's staying. Charlie's trying to persuade Mum to let him stay here . . .'

'We? Who's the we taking Donny out?'

'Me, Mum and Dad, Charlie and Roland.'

Now it was my turn to be jealous. Donny Abreck staying in the same house as Lia. Going out to dinner with Lia. He was bound to fancy her. And he was a regular teen mag pin-up. I felt a dull ache in the pit of my stomach. My biggest fear about Lia was that she would want someone more exciting than me, someone who'd seen more of the world than I had. Someone *exactly* like Donny Abreck. Now she'd met him, she was bound to dump me and go out with him. Maybe she was already planning to, I thought. Normally she would have asked me to go out to dinner with them as well; she liked including me and her mates in whatever was happening. She was really generous like that. But not this time apparently.

Suddenly my great day didn't feel so great anymore.

Celebrity Snog

9

MAC AND I had a good heart-to-heart when I went to pick him up for work the next day.

'Yeah,' he said after I'd filled him in on my day out with Savannah, 'sometimes the best bit about getting off with someone hot is the fact you can tell everyone about it the next day.'

'I didn't get off with her,' I said, as he shut his front door.

'Not yet, you lucky dawg, y'all,' he drawled, in a terrible imitation of a Texan accent.

I tried to hit him but he was too fast for me.

'Only joking,' he said, dodging out of my way. 'But still, way to go. One for the books.'

'I guess,' I said. 'But it was all innocent. Not that Lia believes that.'

'Yeah, sorry I didn't get your message to her. I would

have passed it on if I'd picked it up in time.'

'Not your problem,' I said glumly. 'But maybe you could tell her that I really did leave a message.' Part of me felt that Lia's reaction had been unfair. OK, I had gone off with Savannah for the day; but I hadn't cheated on her and I had *tried* to reach her.

'Will do,' he said, then I guess he must have noticed my miserable expression. 'Hey, don't get down about it. Girls, eh? Who knows what strange things go on in their heads sometimes. She'll come round.'

I shrugged. 'Maybe. Sometimes, though, you just can't win.'

'Don't let it get to you. You need cheering up, mate. Have you heard that joke about the bloke who gets stranded on a desert island?'

I shook my head.

'A castaway called Pete had been all alone on a desert island for years,' he began, 'when he noticed another shipwreck on the horizon. There was only one survivor, a woman, and she was heading his way. He couldn't believe his eyes when he saw who was swimming towards him: Britney Spears. She'd been his pin-up back home before he was shipwrecked. She took one look at him and fell hopelessly in love.

'They spent an idyllic few months making love and walking naked across the beaches. But then one morning,

Pete became withdrawn and unhappy. Britney asked what the matter was. "I'll do anything to make it better," she said. "I know this might seem strange, but would you mind wearing one of my old suits?" he asked. "Course not, darling, whatever makes you happy," she replied and went to put his suit on. This, however, was not enough. "Would you mind cutting your hair short?" he asked. "Whatever it takes," she replied and went to cut her hair. When she returned, he said, "Almost there. Now, would you mind painting a moustache on your face?" She thought it a bit odd, but agreed, saying: "Whatever it takes to make you happy, darling." When she returned, he said, "Perfect, but one final thing. Do you mind if I call you Bert?" "No," she replied, baffled, "go right ahead." Now, grinning from ear to ear and almost back to his happy self, he asked her to stand next to him on the beach and lean against a rock. "Bert," he said. "Wanna beer?" "OK," said Britney. "Bert. You catch the game last Saturday?" "No, I didn't," said Britney. "Bert," he said, "you'll never guess who I've been sleeping with for the last six months . . .'"

I laughed. 'Yeah, right,' I said. 'I get it: men like to show off. But nothing's going to happen between me and Savannah for me to boast about. We held hands, that's all. Like mates. Anyway, I'm going out with Lia. I don't want to blow that.'

'Bec says that Lia was out with Donny Abreck last night.'

'Yeah, but her parents were there as well. Did Becca say anything else about it?'

Mac shook his head. 'Nah, she only had an earful for me.'

'Why's that? What have you done?'

'She reckons I've been flirting with Julie and Chantelle from make-up.'

'She's right,' I said. 'I've seen you.'

'Maybe they've been flirting with me.'

'Haven't seen you objecting, mate.'

Mac shook his head. 'I have to admit it's flattering. And it's made me think. I mean, I like Becca, I really do, but I don't know if I want to . . . you know, be so tied down in a serious relationship at my age. It's like . . . Say Becca is an apple. Great – I like apples. But some days, I might fancy an orange or a melon or another fruit. Like, why stick to one fruit when you can sample the whole basket? It's been great with Becca. It still *is* great, it's just . . . I'd like to be free to flirt around a bit.'

'Then tell her.'

'Pfff. Easier said than done. Don't want to hurt her feelings.'

'I know,' I said. 'But you never know, she may be feeling the same way. I remember when I was going out with Cat and it felt like our relationship had run its course. Neither of us said anything for ages then, when we finally did come clean, we discovered we both felt the same way but were too scared to say anything.'

'I guess that's a possibility,' said Mac, looking unhappy. 'Yeah, I will. I'll talk to her. Are you going to talk to Lia?'

'What about?'

'You and her of course, you dingbat.'

'I don't want to break up with her, so nothing to say at the moment. I want to go out with her. End of story.'

As we rode to work, I wondered if it really was the end of the story. Lia and I had promised always to tell each other the truth and I hadn't let on to her that Savannah had flirted with me. If it meant nothing, I'd have told her and we'd have had a laugh about it. She could trust me, couldn't she? I'm not like Mac, wanting to try every fruit in the basket. Or am I?

As soon as we got to unit base, I reported to the production office to get my list of tasks for the day.

Roland didn't even look up when I knocked on the trailer door. 'Savannah wants to see you, pronto,' he said.

'Errands?'

Roland shrugged and began to dial a number on his phone. 'Dunno, she didn't say. Better get over there.'

I was dying to ask him about his evening out with Lia and the others, but I didn't want to give him the slightest notion that I was worried. I had thought about phoning Lia and simply asking her how it had been, but then she might feel I was crowding her or acting desperate after our last uncomfortable phone call. Be cool, I kept telling myself. Be cool.

Five minutes later, I was anything but cool. My heart was beating fast in my chest and I got the distinct feeling I was blushing as red as Savannah's hair. And I'm not a blusher normally. I was with her in her trailer, and she didn't want errands running. Oh, no. She wanted to rehearse a scene from the film. With me taking the other actor's part. And it wasn't just any old scene she wanted to go through. It was a snogging scene.

Oh. My. God.

'But why don't you wait and do it with Donny?' I asked.

'Him? Hah! I've worked with him before and if you wait for him to show up, you wait all day. No, it's a crucial scene. I want to get it right.'

'Then . . . why don't you get one of the other actors in?' I stuttered. 'I mean I . . .'

'I tried Bill and I tried Jake but they've both got some kind of throat infection that's going round. I can't risk

catching it. Why? Y'all got a problem with this, Squidge?'
She raised an eyebrow and looked at me with an amused
expression.

'Er, no, course not, er . . . just . . . How about Roland?
He's more senior than me.'

Savannah rolled her eyes in exasperation. 'I'm prepared to
suffer for my art to a certain degree, but, dahlin', I ain't prepared
to go *that* far. Hey, come on. Some people would pay good
money for an opportunity like this. What's the problem?'

'No problem. Honest.'

'You worried about your girlfriend, Mia?'

'Lia.'

'Whatever. Hey, come on, Squidge, get real here. It's
only acting. It's not like you're being unfaithful.'

Hmm, not sure Lia would see it that way, I thought. But
then, how can I say no? I'll look like a total amateur. I want
to work in films. If I was on my own set, I'd muck in where
necessary. Plus, the idea was tempting, very tempting. It
was a way of snogging Savannah without really being
disloyal to Lia. It would be acting. I decided to be
professional and detach myself from my feelings. It was
only a job. I'd do the scene.

After I'd agreed, she gave me a copy of the script and
I had a quick read through of the scene she wanted to go
over. It was the part where Pip meets up with Estella in

London when they're older and she teases him and plays with his feelings. *Great Expectations* was one of my favourite books when I was younger and I'd read it a few times so I knew that the scriptwriter had used some poetic licence. I couldn't remember there being an actual snogging scene in the book at that stage of the story, but then each writer and director interprets things differently. From a director's point of view, I could understand exactly why a kiss had been written in. Savannah and Donny's fans would expect it. And the producers would love it, as they could use the scene to promote the film.

'Ready?' asked Savannah.

I gulped, nodded and read my lines out loud. After a few moments, I got into it and it felt good. Then I came to the part of the script that read:

Estella leans forward, brushes Pip's hair from his face and kisses him lightly on the lips. She pulls back, then Pip moves forward and kisses her more deeply, almost greedily.

Gulp. OK, I thought, get ready. God, I wish I'd known I was going to have to do this, I would have sucked mints for an hour or two beforehand. I'd read in a magazine somewhere that one actress hated kissing her leading man as he always tasted of garlic or onions. What did I have for breakfast? Was it Marmite? People either love it or hate it. No, it wasn't Marmite, it was . . .

Oh God, Savannah, I mean Estella, was leaning forward. My mind went into overdrive. It was like there was this mad voice gabbling away in the back of my head, telling me that I had to stay in character, as that way I wouldn't be cheating on Lia because it wasn't me kissing Savannah, it was Pip kissing Estella, and he's not me, I'm not him and she's not her. Oh God, oo *oo* – Savannah's lips were on mine. A fleeting kiss. Gentle. My stomach did a backflip. Nice.

She moved back and looked at me, waiting. It was my turn. I am Pip; I am Pip. What's my motivation? I am intimidated by Estella, I thought, trying to remember the story. Never mind Estella; I'm intimidated by *Savannah*. This is real. No, it's not real. It's acting. I glanced down at the script. Pip moves in and kisses her more deeply. OK. Right. I can do this, I thought. I took a deep breath. Swallowed. Looked up at Savannah. Grinned like an idiot.

'No, *no*,' she said, with an impatient wave of her hand. 'Get in the mood. Pip wouldn't smile. This is an *intense* moment. A moment he's dreamed about for years. All his life, he's adored Estella, put her on a pedestal. This is the moment he's been waiting for.'

'Right,' I said. 'Got you.' Actually I *can* do this, I

thought. What Savannah had described was exactly how I'd felt about Lia for months before we got together. I'll imagine that I'm reliving that first kiss with Lia.

Savannah leaned over and gave me her fleeting kiss again then pulled back.

Think about Lia, I told myself. Imagine this is Lia and it's that first time I ever got to kiss her. I leaned over, looked into Estella's eyes, closed my eyes then kissed her.

And she kissed me back. But it didn't feel like Lia kissing me back. No, of course it wouldn't, I thought. This is Estella. Woah, a very *passionate* Estella. I don't think it mentioned kissing with tongues in the script but I was definitely getting Estella's, I mean Savannah's, I mean Lia's. Oh *God*, who am I kissing here? How long is this kiss meant to go on for? And *woah*, it feels really good.

I pulled back and opened my eyes. As I did, I swear I saw a flash at the window. A camera flash.

Savannah gasped. 'Who was that?'

I ran to the window and just glimpsed the shape of a man disappearing behind one of the trailers.

I opened the trailer door and ran out after whoever it was but, too late, he was gone.

Savannah came and stood behind me. 'Hell,' she said. 'I hope that wasn't the press. They bug me wherever I am these days. Always looking for a story. It's one *almighty* drag.'

And it *will* be one almighty drag if that kiss gets back to Lia, I thought, as Julie and Chantelle from the make-up department walked past, took a good long look at us then giggled. Chantelle turned back and winked at me.

10 Flower Girls

GOSSIP ABOUT my trip to Fowey with Savannah had spread round the unit base like a Mexican wave at a football match. And of course, it had also got to Cat, Becca . . . and Lia, who had come to hang out with the girls in their break.

'Here comes the toy boy,' teased Becca, when I found them hanging out at the back of the trailers and taking in the good weather we were having. 'Heard that you've got a new job as an escort now.'

I looked closely at the three of them and tried to gauge what was going on in their heads. Toy boy? Was Becca being snide? Had she and Cat been talking and sided with Lia, casting me as the villain? I decided to keep things light and smiled back at Becca. 'Yep, it was a tough job but someone had to do it. Riding in a limo, sightseeing, hanging out with a celeb. Yeah, it was *really* hard work.'

Cat and Becca smiled back at me but Lia didn't.

'So what's she like?' asked Cat.

'Nice,' I said. 'Sweet. A bit lonely.'

'Everyone thinks she fancies you,' said Becca.

'Well who could blame her?' I said, laughing. 'Nah, I think she just wants someone to talk to.'

'That's not what's being said around here,' said Becca. 'Some people have almost got you married off.'

I shrugged and directed my reply to Lia. 'Yeah, but you can't believe everything you hear. And you must know what it's like from when your dad was on the road and in the public eye, Lia. He told me about being on tour and people reading too much into situations that were totally innocent.'

At that moment, Fran, the lady in charge of catering, beckoned Cat and Becca to go back into work. So, at last, I was left alone with Lia.

'So are you going to tell me what's really going on?' she asked.

I took her hand and squeezed it in what I hoped was a reassuring manner. Lia winced. Clearly I'd squeezed too hard.

'Nothing,' I said. 'Honest. If anything had been going on when we went down to Fowey, I wouldn't have told you that I'd spent the day with her, would I? I could have said that I was over in Plymouth on my own. Surely the fact that

I told you that I'd been with Savannah as soon as I got back means that nothing went on?'

Lia considered what I'd said for a moment. 'So what you're saying is, if something was going on between you and Savannah, then you wouldn't tell me?'

'Yes. *NO*,' I was getting confused. 'No, what I was saying was because I told you that I'd spent the day with her, it means that I *am* telling you what has been going on. Which is nothing. When people cheat, they don't tend to tell their girlfriend or boyfriend *anything* about their actions.'

It wasn't coming out right at all. And I hadn't told her about the rehearsal I'd just done with Savannah or the kiss, or the photo. Why was that? I asked myself. Is it because something *is* going on? But it isn't. Not really. So maybe I should tell her. But would she be upset? Sometimes what you don't know, doesn't hurt you. God, I don't know. It's not half confusing.

'How do I know if I can trust you, Squidge?' she asked, but at the same moment, Sandra appeared from behind the trailer.

'Hey, Squidge. Roland's looking for you,' she said. 'He said to make it snappy.'

'Right. OK. See you later, Lia.'

'Yeah,' she said. 'Later.'

She's still not happy with me, I thought, as I made my

way over to see Roland. How am I going to put this right? I do want to keep seeing her. I do want her to be my girlfriend. Trying to explain in words doesn't work; in fact, explanations only seem to land me more in trouble. How can I let her know how much I care?

When I got to the production office, I saw that Donny Abreck was in there with Roland and Sandra. In case he was saying something private, I didn't go straight in. Instead, I hovered on the steps from where I could hear Donny ranting and raving inside. It was weird listening to him. He was expressing the part of me that feels restricted living here in Cornwall.

'This place is the boons. It's like . . . it's like the edge of the world,' moaned Donny. 'There's nothing to do, there's no movie house, no shops, no restaurants . . .'

'You're only here a few days,' I heard Sandra say. 'We'll make your scenes top priority, then you'll be out of here.'

What is his problem? I asked myself. As Sandra was saying, he doesn't have to stay here forever. Unlike me, who's had to spend his whole life in the place. He's with us for a week, tops, then he's out of here. Surely part of the job of being an actor is going where the job demands.

Then Donny began a long list of all his personal requirements: can't eat this, won't eat that; must have this, mustn't have that. I could see that there was going to be a lot of running around after him while he was on the set. What a prat, I thought. Who does he think he is? I decided to nickname him Primadonny because of the way he was carrying on.

When I'm a director, I decided, I'm going to give all sorts of unknown actors parts. Actors who will appreciate getting the work and won't moan when they have to go to a quiet location for a week or so. Sometimes we see the same old faces over and over again in films, when there's a whole army of good actors out there all waiting for their break. Actors who wouldn't behave like spoiled kids. Savannah's not like that. Not when you get to know her. She hadn't objected to the location, not once. In fact, like in Fowey on Saturday, she's taking this as a chance to see a world that's different to the one she lives in. And all that stuff that Roland came out with about her not wanting to mix with the crew. Rubbish – she's been really cool with everyone.

'And the hotel I'm in,' continued Donny. 'The corridors creak, the plumbing rattles, my room smells of boiled vegetables and there's no goddamn shower. How do people here keep clean?'

'The Axford's have kindly said that you can stay with them,' said Sandra. 'I take it that you want to move?'

'You bet. I was out with them Saturday night. Nice folk, the Axfords. Have my things moved over as soon as possible.'

He came out and almost walked into me.

'Oops,' I said, dodging out of his way.

He didn't even glance at me. He just kept walking as though I wasn't there. When he'd gone, I stepped into the trailer. Roland handed me a list. I glanced down at it. The usual white lilies for Savannah. And a whole load of stuff for Donny.

'Be sure to get the shampoo because he's run out,' said Roland pointing to an item at the bottom of the list then handing me an empty shampoo bottle. '*Être*, it's called. Take the bottle so you don't get it wrong. It's some French type that everybody in Hollywood uses. If you can't get any, order it. Oh, and get me a bottle as well.'

I made my way over to my bike. It was a good job that my dad had fixed a box on the back for carrying things, as there was going to be a lot to bring back.

I left my bike at Arthur's pub and took the ferry over to Plymouth, then a bus into town. As soon as I got there, I tried a couple of the big pharmacies for Donny's shampoo, but no luck; they had a million other varieties but not his. After trying a dozen smaller chemists and hairdressers, there was nowhere else to try. Maybe it's no longer available, I thought, as I came out of the last place I could think of, at least, not down here. I can't go back empty handed though. Maybe he'll settle for something else. I made my way back to the first place I'd tried and perused the shelves. They heaved with every type of product for every type of hair. I chose a posh designer one by a celebrity hairdresser and hoped that it would do the trick. I bought an extra bottle for Roland.

After that, I bought the other things on Donny's list, then headed for the flower market for Savannah's lilies. The market was held in a vast old warehouse down by the water in the Old Town. The air smelt sweet and fresh as I stepped inside. The place was a riot of colour: reds, purples, pinks, yellows, oranges; there were flowers of every shade, shape and size.

As I headed for the white lilies, my thoughts turned to what Mac had said this morning about different girls being like different fruits. I'd compare them to different flowers, I thought, as I took in all the types on display. For one thing, there are more varieties of flower than fruit and they have more subtle associations to describe the thousands of different types of girl out there. I mean, with fruit, you're limited. And who would ever want to be compared to a pear or a grapefruit? It's not poetic, somehow. Imagine a romantic evening and looking into a girl's eyes and saying, 'Hey, you remind me of a banana'. She'd probably hit you. But if you said, 'You remind me of a rose in bloom', or something soppy like that, she'd probably like it. Yeah, I thought, I must remember to tell Mac that flowers are far better than fruit for comparing girls to.

I'd never thought about it before, but there must be the perfect flower here to compare to a hundred different girls. What would Lia be? I cast my eye around the flowers on display. No, not those purple ones over there, nor those pink ones there, definitely not a daffodil. Something elegant, graceful – like her. Maybe a white rose? No, they are lovely, but too common. Then I saw the perfect flower: an orchid – white with a pale pink centre. It was exquisite. Beautiful, just like her. Yes, that's it, I decided. Lia would be a rare orchid.

And what would Savannah be? I asked myself, as I made my way to the lily section. I soon spotted it. Savannah may like her white lilies, I thought, but that's not what she'd be. No, she'd be . . . I bent to read the label on the bucket. Tiger lily, it said. That's it. She'd be a tiger lily. Bright orange. In your face. Can't miss it.

I glanced at my watch and realised that I should be heading back to get the ferry. I quickly went to the white lilies.

'Been a naughty boy then, have you?' said the flower seller, with a knowing look when I went to pay for the required three dozen.

'What do you mean?' I asked.

The man nodded to the flowers. 'Three dozen! To buy a bouquet that size, you have to have done *something*.'

I laughed as I handed over the money. 'Not me, mate. I'm innocent.'

'Yeah, right,' said the flower man, with a wink. 'Aren't we all?'

I gave him a cheesy grin back as I took the lilies. I guess he must see a lot of blokes in here buying flowers to make up with their wives or girlfriends, I thought. I wonder if it works.

As I walked out of the market and back towards the bus stop, there were a couple of girls walking towards me on the opposite side of the pavement.

'Those for me?' one of them called over, giving me a big smile.

'Next time,' I called back. I was feeling good. My jobs were all done. I felt just in the mood for a bit of harmless banter.

Through the window of a hairdressing salon, a receptionist spotted me and called her friend over. They started waving at me and pointing to the flowers then putting their hands over their hearts and laughing. I laughed back. Hmm, I thought, I've bought flowers before for Mum and for relatives' birthdays, but I've *never* had a reaction like this before. Obviously the bigger the bunch, the better. That's it! I thought. That's how I'll show Lia that I care. I quickly added up how much I'd saved so far since I'd started working. It had to be an impressive bouquet for Lia, at least as stunning as the one I had for Savannah. A half-dead cheapo bunch from a corner shop certainly wouldn't do the trick. No, but a huge bunch will tell her what I can't say with words. It will be worth the cost and I can make up the money later. Yes, flowers. They will be loads better than a thousand explanations, apologies or excuses about the rehearsal and why I'd kissed Savannah.

I turned on my heel and headed back for the market, where I picked out a dozen orchids. I almost passed out when I heard how much they cost.

'You *sure* you haven't done anything?' asked the flower man as I handed over the money for the second bouquet.

I shook my head. 'Nope, but you know how it is with girls – you can't tell *them* that, so best buy them flowers.'

The man tapped the side of his nose. 'You're a wise man,' he said. 'A wise man.'

11

Operation Shampoo

DONNY WAS OK with his shampoo when I took it to him on my return to unit base. Though I did have to explain that it wasn't any old shampoo – that a celebrity hairdresser created it. Roland wasn't happy; he wanted *Être* and only *Être*. He wanted the product used by the stars, and nothing else would do.

'Is this *Être* or is this some cheapo product that any Jo Blow uses?' he asked, when I offered him the bottle of the same shampoo I'd bought for Donny.

For God's sake, it's only shampoo, I thought. But Roland wasn't having it and sent me out again to find him some. No problem, I thought. I'd find the stuff if it meant that much to him, even if it meant researching it on the Internet and him having to wait weeks to get it. I'd get him a bumper bottle! I felt on top of the world and nothing, not even Roland, could dampen my mood. I'd been on cloud nine since I'd seen Lia and given her the flowers.

On the ferry coming back from Plymouth, I'd phoned Lia on my mobile and asked if she could meet me for a late lunch. She'd agreed and was totally blown away when I gave her the orchids and told her my new theory about women and flowers and how I thought she was like a rare orchid. I must remember this for the future, I thought, as she gave me a huge snog. Flowers can buy you loads of brownie points.

But it wasn't just the flowers. Mac had let her know that I'd tried to reach her from Fowey and had left a message on his voicemail and her mum had also told her that I'd tried to reach her. I think she was feeling guilty about having been so cool with me.

After a good bit of making-up kissing, we had a great lunch-break, sitting outside the pub, eating chips, catching up and having a laugh and a gossip about everyone on the set. We were an item again and nothing and no one could touch us. Not Roland. (She was appalled when I admitted I was worried she might fancy him.) Not Donny. ('Not my type,' she'd said. 'Too full of himself.') I really wanted to tell her about the rehearsal kiss with Savannah and the mystery photographer, but I chickened out when she apologised for the fifth time about not trusting me more. Things had only just got back to normal with us and I didn't want to risk ruining a perfect moment.

I will tell her, I *will* tell her, I told myself, as I rode back to the set after we'd parted. I'll tell her when the time is right. In the meantime, I still had to find Roland's shampoo. I'd exhausted all the likely places to find *Être* in Plymouth so thought that the best thing was to get out the phone book and call every salon and pharmacist listed to see if I could buy it anywhere in the South West. I called every salon between Portsmouth and Bristol, but they all gave me the same story.

'Sorry, love, *Être* isn't available anymore.'

'Nope, they stopped making it months ago.'

I didn't like to go back to unit base and admit failure, but by five o'clock I had no choice; there wasn't anywhere else to try.

Roland didn't like it. He was in the office with Sandra when I got back and gave him the bad news.

'It's only to be expected when you hire a kid as a runner I guess,' he said to her, not even giving me a second glance.

'But it's no longer available,' I said, determined to get him to at least acknowledge my presence.

At last he turned and looked at me. 'Listen, no longer available is not acceptable. Come back with an answer like that and you wouldn't last a minute in Hollywood.'

What would you know? I thought. You're just a jumped-up Boy Scout who never got to be pack leader. I'd show him who wouldn't last in Hollywood. I'd track down a bottle of his precious shampoo if it killed me.

First stop was the local hairdresser to ask her to check suppliers further afield than the South West. Luckily, she happens to be my mum. I told her what I was looking for.

'Never heard of *Être*, love,' she said. 'But ring our Pat in Leicester; she supplies all the major salons and posh shops in London. She might have heard of it.'

Two minutes later, I had Auntie Pat on the phone.

'Just a sec,' she said. 'I'll look it up on my computer. Yep, here it is. *Être*. No, it's not French at all. It's made in Scunthorpe. Factory went out of business last month.'

'Is there any way you can get me a bottle? Do they have old stocks for sale?'

'Not that I can see. Why does it have to be *Être*?'

'It's for one of the production team here. He's a bit of a prat and wants to use the same designer products as the stars.'

Auntie Pat laughed. 'Then more fool him. The base of most shampoo is usually the same, what makes it all appear different is the scent added and then the packaging. And that's all you pay for with the top-of-the-range stuff – the packaging.'

That gave me an idea. I still had Donny's empty bottle in the box on the back of my bike so dashed out to get it. I ran up to the bathroom and poured in a measure of the economy shampoo that Mum gets from the supermarket, then I rifled through Mum's selection of essential oils that she keeps by the bath. The sandalwood smelled pretty exotic. A few drops of that, a splash of orange and, *voilà* . . . *Être*, Squidge style.

I quickly whizzed back to unit base and Roland.

'Got you the last bottle in existence,' I said putting the bottle on the desk in front of him. 'It's your lucky day, mate.'

It was hysterical when I reported to him the next morning. He was looking at himself in the small mirror on the wall behind his desk. He ran his fingers through his hair. 'Worth every penny, that stuff,' he said. 'And it smells amazing. You can always tell quality. I can see why everyone's using it.'

I smiled back. 'Yeah, right.'

He must have been really pleased with me because, for once, I wasn't sent off to Plymouth or to the village on mad errands. Instead I was told to report up to the main house, where the crew were shooting a couple of scenes between Herbert Pocket and Pip.

'Jenny, the continuity girl, has phoned in with food poisoning,' said Roland, 'and I can't find anyone to cover. Now, do you know what continuity is?'

I nodded. Boy, did I know. The job of a continuity person is to keep track of how things look from scene to scene and make sure nothing has been changed unless it's meant to have been. Sounds easy but the average film has over two hundred scenes in it and those scenes are often shot out of sequence then put together in the right order by the director and editor at the end. Mistakes often happen. They're called bloopers and spotting them or reading about them is one of my favourite pastimes.

There are some brilliant web sites listing the famous ones. According to my favourite site, *Titanic* has one hundred and eighty five bloopers. In *Harry Potter and the Philosopher's Stone*, there were one hundred and forty one. In *Lord of the Rings: The Fellowship of the Ring*, one hundred and nineteen. I have my personal favourites, like during the filming of *Bonfire of the Vanities*, Melanie Griffiths allegedly had a boob job. So, because they filmed out of sequence, her boobs go from normal to huge and back again all the way through the film. And probably the most famous movie mistake of all time occurs during the famous chariot race scene in *Ben Hur*, when you can clearly see that one of the charioteers is wearing a wrist watch. Not quite right for ancient times. I suppose I'm a bit of an anorak when it comes to collecting examples. So, yes, I know about continuity and bloopers but I wasn't going to let on to Roland just how much, in case he thought I was being a smarmy know it all.

'So, your job is to watch the props from scene to scene,' said Roland. 'In particular, to keep an eye on the food and drink levels. You do understand, don't you?'

'You can count on me. I know what to do,' I said.

I raced up to the house and took my place at the back of the room, where the sound and lighting technicians were just finishing rigging everything up. I made a mental note of the set up. I looked over at the actors. Donny was there and some actor I didn't recognise, who was playing Herbert. I looked at how they were dressed. I quickly scanned their wrists in case either of them had forgotten to remove a digital wrist watch – I didn't reckon that they had them in Dickens' time. Did either of them have a handkerchief protruding from a pocket or anything else that might get used or changed if there were any retakes? I studied the table where they were going to be eating: china cups – they would be OK as no one could see the level of liquid in them; a bowl of fruit including grapes and a couple of apples; slices of bread on a plate. Best keep a close eye on those items, I thought.

Charlie was busy on the other side of the room, talking to some of her crew and she looked over at me and waved. I waved back. It felt great to be there, at the heart of it all, a part of the action instead of running around getting people grocery supplies. *This* was what I'd signed up for.

'Where's the spare fruit and bread?' I asked Sandra, as she hurried past. She pointed to a table behind the cameras. 'There's a whole load over there,' she said. 'Enough fresh fruit and bread to do seventy retakes.'

I gave her the thumbs up.

Charlie said 'Action' and the two actors went into their scene. Pip said his lines in between taking bites out of an apple then he had a bite of one of the pieces of bread. Herbert drank out of one of the cups and ate a few grapes. It was a short scene, only a couple of lines, and didn't take long to do.

'Let's run that again,' said Charlie, positioning herself to shoot the same scene from another angle.

'Props,' called Sandra.

I whizzed straight in and replaced the eaten apple with a new one, the bread with a new slice and the grapes with a bunch that hadn't been touched.

Charlie shouted, 'Action,' again and the actors did their scene a second time.

'OK, let's move on,' said Charlie when they'd finished.

The actors went into the next scene, where Herbert leaves the room and Pip is left alone. I was really enjoying watching. Charlie was a stickler for perfection and made the actors do scene after scene, again and again. She shot each scene from a few different angles so that later she could edit it so that the audience saw Pip's reaction to Herbert, then Herbert's reaction to Pip. She then announced that she wanted to redo the first scene again. I was about to dive in again with untouched fruit and bread when Roland appeared behind me.

'You're needed outside,' he said. 'I'll take over here.'

'But . . .' I pointed at the breakfast table.

'Next scenes we're shooting are exteriors. I need you at the bottom of the drive. Make sure that there are no cars or motorbikes ready to motor in and ruin the film.'

'OK,' I said. 'But Charlie wants to redo the first scene and the fruit needs replacing. Oh, and one slice of bread.'

Roland gave me a disdainful look. 'I do *know* how it works,' he said.

'Wasn't saying you didn't,' I said. 'Just thought you'd like to know where we're up to.'

'Just get your butt outside and clear the area,' he said.

So much for team spirit, I thought, but no problem. I went outside. One of the production assistants who was busy getting things in motion showed me where to go. She pointed down the driveway and I went and stood guard at the end of the road leading to the location where the next scene was to take place. The lighting technicians were hard at it again and the production assistants were busy running round ensuring that everything was in its proper place. It's amazing how many people are needed to make a movie, I thought, as I watched the crew buzz about doing their various tasks. Seeing them all in action, it was obvious that every one of the people on that long list of names that you see at the end of a film was needed.

A few stray cars tried to drive up as I stood at my post but most people were only too happy to drive back or take another route, so my job was relatively easy. Then a red Fiesta drove up.

'Oi, you, the ugly git with the spiky hair,' shouted the man at the wheel. 'What you filming?'

I grinned as I recognised my cousin Roger. Ever since we were little, we've acted mad with each other, slagging each other off and seeing who could come up with the best insult. I indicated a group of extras standing waiting at the far end of the drive, all of whom were in period costume ready for the next scene. 'Clearly nothing that needs a red Fiesta in the background, you dingbat,' I called back to him. 'Now get lost and don't come back.'

Roger made a rude gesture, so I made one back. Then he

reversed his car and drove away. It was then that I noticed that Roland and Sandra had come out of the main house and were standing a short distance to my left. Roland had a face like thunder.

'Don't you *ever* speak to a member of the public like that again,' he shouted.

'But . . . he's my cousin,' I explained. 'My cousin Roger. We were having a laugh.' Sadly, Roland didn't see it that way.

'Your behaviour was totally unprofessional,' he said as Sandra looked on. 'Other people around don't know that he's your cousin and that would have been seen as a display of appalling rudeness.'

'But there's nobody around,' I objected. 'Not within hearing distance, only you and Sandra.'

Sandra looked embarrassed for me. *I* felt embarrassed for me. Why did he have to give me a dressing down in front of her? It made me look stupid. So much for the shampoo, I thought. Getting on his good side was obviously a waste of time. It hadn't taken very long for him to turn on me again.

'I'll take over here – you're obviously incompetent,' said Roland dismissing me with a wave of his hand.

'So what should I do next?' I asked.

Just at that moment, Charlie came out on to the steps of the house. 'Hold on the exteriors,' she said, looking up at the sky, which was beginning to darken. 'Damn, I hope it's not going to rain.'

'What's the problem?' I heard Sandra ask.

Charlie looked over at me. 'Props. We need to redo the first scenes. The fruit doesn't match the later scenes on one of the retakes – it's already been eaten – so the continuity's all wrong. God, I hate it when this happens. It wastes so much time.' She glanced up at the sky again. 'I just pray this dry weather will last another hour.'

Roland looked over at me accusingly.

I wasn't having it. 'It wasn't me,' I said. 'I watched *every* scene, *every* mouthful that was eaten and drunk. It was all in the right place. For that first scene, I made sure that the food looked untouched every time.'

'Well it wasn't me,' said Roland.

Charlie gave us both a weary look then went back inside.

I felt angry. I knew it was him that had blown it and he wasn't big enough to admit it. I *knew* that I'd matched each piece of fruit, every slice of bread for every scene.

'So what do you want me to do?' I asked.

'What do you think you *can* do without getting it wrong? I don't know. Go and get a weather forecast, then report back.'

It was pretty obvious that the outlook didn't look good, but I got out of there fast. I felt ready to hit him.

It didn't take a moment to do as he'd asked, I simply

rang the twenty-four-hour weather line. It said that there would be rain later.

'You go and tell Charlie,' said Roland. 'Seeing as it was you who held her up.'

'Was not,' I said. But I went back into the house to find Charlie and give her the news. I waited to one side as she was busy shooting the retakes, then I told her about the weather. It might have been my imagination but she wasn't as friendly to me as she normally was. I felt rotten. Maybe she didn't believe that it wasn't me who'd messed things up. But at least there would be no damage done. She'd spotted the incontinuity and had reshot. She might just be able to regain the time lost.

The retakes took another twenty minutes, then the action moved outside. Roland was down at the end of the location and didn't seem in a hurry to give me my next job, so I decided to hang around and watch what was going on. It looked as though the light might hold, so everything might turn out all right. I hoped that it would.

Things got going and the scene was in full swing when the second disaster happened. The location looked great. The light was great. The costumes looked fabulous. The actors were delivering their lines brilliantly. The extras were milling around busily in the background. Charlie was filming away happily and it looked like everything was back on track.

Then there was the most almighty roar. Everyone looked up to see a formation of jets fly overhead. Not quite the right effect for the turn of the century!

'*Noooooo*,' I heard Charlie cry in exasperation.

Everything came to a standstill as we waited for the sound to subside as the jets disappeared into the distance.

'Right, we're going to have to go again,' said Charlie. 'Damn, and we almost had it in the bag. Roland, we knew that these air displays happen down here from time to time. I asked you to research where and when. How did this one escape your attention? It would have been advertised, surely?'

Roland sighed and pointed to me. 'I *am* sorry, Charlie. I asked that kid you hired to do it.'

This time I saw red. 'No way. You never did, Roland. That's a blatant lie!'

'See,' said Roland. 'This is what I've had to deal with from day one. I didn't want to bother you with it, but he's really not up to the job, Charlie. And now it's having an effect on the movie . . .'

'So deal with it,' said Charlie impatiently. 'I haven't got time for petty disagreements; we're running over schedule. OK, places everyone. Let's go again.'

I felt outraged as people began to look at me with disdain. They obviously believed Roland and thought I'd ruined the continuity in the breakfast scene and now I was responsible for an eight-jet flyover. I opened my mouth to protest again but Charlie had started filming.

And then the third disaster happened: another roar came from the sky, but this time it wasn't jet planes. It was thunder. Then there was a flash of lightning and the skies opened. A downpour of torrential rain which soaked the set in seconds. Cameramen desperately covered their cameras, the actors and the rest of the crew ran to shelter in the porch of the house. Suddenly the location was empty.

No doubt I'm going to be blamed for the deluge as well, I thought, as I took shelter under a tree with the rain soaking through my T-shirt. Well, at least things can't get any worse, I thought as I turned away and trudged down the drive, away from the action and the angry glances of the cast and crew.

Paparazzi

12

I WAS AWOKEN the next morning by a loud shriek coming from downstairs. I leaped out of bed to go and see what was going on and a quick glance at my watch told me that I had overslept. Oh *no*, I thought, as I grabbed my jeans from the floor and staggered into them. It was ten minutes past eight and I was supposed to have been on site at eight. Roland would kill me. I got out into the hall at the same time as Dad and Will appeared from their bedrooms.

'What's the matter?' asked Dad, poking his head over the banister.

'This,' said Mum waving the morning paper in the air. She got her glasses out of her dressing gown pocket for a closer look. 'Our Squidge is on the front cover!'

Dad, Will and I charged downstairs and stood over her as she read out the headline: *Local boy in celebrity love fest.*

'Wahey,' said Will gawking at the photo of Savannah and I in her trailer, mid-snog. 'You never said you'd got off with her!'

'I didn't,' I said. 'We were rehearsing . . .'

'That's a good one,' chuckled Dad. 'Not heard that before.'

'It's true,' I said. 'Oh God, Lia.'

'Bit late to be thinking of Lia by the looks of it,' said Dad, as he attempted to read over Mum's shoulder.

'What does it say?' I asked.

Mum pushed her glasses up her nose and read from the paper. 'Pipped at the post. Celebrity actress, Savannah (17), finds love amongst the locals. Savannah, who is currently starring in the production of *Great Expectations* being filmed at Mount Edgecumbe, was seen with local boy, Jack Squires, in the seaside resort of Fowey. They were later spotted in Savannah's trailer getting up close and personal. Savannah's management were unavailable for comment but local girls say that Jack, known as Squidge, has always been popular with the girls and has a reputation as a love rat.'

I had to laugh at that. Me, a love rat? I've only ever kissed three girls: Cat, Lia, and Savannah.

Mum peered over her glasses at me. 'Looks like you've got some explaining to do, mi lad.'

I nodded and ran upstairs to find my mobile and grab my fleece. Then I was out the door, and on my way to work.

But first I had to ring Lia.

I stopped in a quiet lane and dialled her mobile. It was switched off, so I tried the land line.

Her mum picked up. 'She's gone into town with Zac and Donny for the morning. Do you want to leave a message?'

'Message?' Somehow I felt that asking Lia's mum if she'd seen the photo of me snogging Savannah was inappropriate. Surely she'd have said something if she had. 'Er, er, no,' I replied. Leave a message? What would I say? What if there were other people around when Lia's mum passed it on? No, I decided, I'd rather speak to her in person, when she was on her own.

'Are you OK, Squidge?' asked Mrs Axford. 'You sound a bit strange.'

'Yes, fine, er . . . you haven't by any chance seen today's paper have you?'

'Not yet, why?'

'Oh, nothing. Um, please could you just tell Lia that I called.'

'Will do.'

When I arrived at unit base, Roland was hovering outside the production office like a wasp waiting to sting.

'You're late,' he said, looking at his watch.

'I know. Sorry, I . . .'

'What's the first commandment on a film set?' he asked.

Thou shalt always obey Roland Rat, I thought to myself. 'Remember we're a team?' I said hopefully.

'Wrong: time is money.'

'Right,' I said. 'I'm sorry, I really, *really* am. I overslept, then there was, er . . .'

Roland produced the morning paper from behind his back. 'Don't worry, I've seen it. Everyone's seen it. And you're fired.'

'What? For kissing Savannah? But, she asked me to. We were rehearsing.'

'Not just that. For being late today. For all the cock-ups yesterday.'

'But none of them were my fault . . .'

'No room for buts on a film set,' he said. 'In this case, your butt.'

'But surely Charlie . . .'

'Mrs Bennett to you. Anyway, you heard her yesterday. She told me to deal with it – it being you – and I have.' Then he turned back into the production office and closed the door firmly behind him.

I was about to go in after him and plead my case but I stopped. No point, I thought. He's been waiting for this day since the moment he set eyes on me. There's only one person who can help put this straight, and that's Savannah.

I made my way over to her trailer and knocked. There was nobody there.

As I was coming back down the steps, Chantelle walked past. 'Savannah's not in there,' she said.

'Where has she gone?' I asked.

Chantelle shrugged, then winked. 'Maybe she's gone looking for love amongst the locals.'

'Yeah, very funny,' I said.

'Actually, I think she may have left. I think she did the last of her scenes the day before yesterday.'

I sat on the steps and put my head in my hands. Savannah, gone? Maybe she didn't see the paper. Or maybe she did and went into hiding. I wouldn't blame her, but I'd thought we were friends. At least she could have said goodbye.

'Hey you,' said a friendly voice to my right.

I looked up.

It was Mac. 'You look down in the dumps,' he said, sitting down next to me.

'Just been fired.'

'Ah, for snogging Savannah?'

'For that and for daring to breathe the same air as Roland. So you've seen the paper?'

Mac nodded. 'Fame at last. Um, probably not what you wanted, eh? Tough luck. But best not sit here with that long face. It looks like you're pining for Savannah.'

'Chantelle said she may have gone.'

Mac nodded. 'Yeah, Becca said she'd split.'

'Have you spoken to Lia?' I asked.

He shook his head. 'Bec said she's out for the morning with her dad and Donny. She doesn't know if Lia's seen the paper. What are you going to do?'

'Try and explain. Put things right. What a mess.'

Mac put his hand on my arm. 'Yeah.' Then he laughed. 'Love rat.'

'That's a joke,' I said. 'I've only ever snogged three girls.'

'Well, don't let anyone else know that. Having a reputation as a love rat can do wonders for your babe magnetism.'

'Really?'

'Yeah, girls always love a bad boy. They like the challenge of being the one to tame them.'

'But the only girl I'm interested in is Lia. She's going to kill me if, or rather when, she sees that newspaper.'

'Not your day is it?'

'Not my week. I'd almost saved enough to replace my camcorder, as well. Would have done, in fact, if I hadn't forked out for the flowers for Lia. I guess they were a total waste of money.'

'Maybe not. You don't know how she's going to react to the piece in the paper. And she was really knocked out by the flowers. Becca told me that she thought you were the most sensitive boy she'd ever met.'

'Really?'

'Yeah,' said Mac. 'On a par with Dawson from *Dawson's Creek*.'

'Dawson?' I pulled a face. 'Mr Sensitive. Oh, double yuck. He's so *wet*. I'm not *that* wet. Oh, please. Oh, God, my life is over.'

Mac started laughing. 'OK, maybe not on a par with Dawson – I made that bit up. You could never be that wet. But Lia did say that she thought you were sensitive. Anyway, the newspaper story. How are you going to get out of that? I mean, you did kiss Savannah. No doubt about that.'

'Yeah, but she *asked* me to. She wanted to rehearse a scene from the movie and Donny wasn't around. It was innocent. It really *really* was.'

'What was it like?'

'*Mac* . . .'

'Oh, come on. I'd tell *you*.'

'Well . . . Pretty hot actually,' I said. 'But it was innocent on my part, honestly. I even tried to pretend that I was kissing Lia, so that it wouldn't be cheating.'

Mac cracked up laughing at that. 'So how come you didn't tell me?'

'I wanted to tell Lia first. And I was going to, I really

was. I was just waiting for the right time. Plus, I didn't think you'd believe that it was innocent.'

Mac squeezed my arm. 'I believe you, mate. Thousands wouldn't.'

I grimaced. 'I just hope that Lia isn't one of those thousands.'

Reject

13

I DIDN'T hang around at unit base after I'd finished talking to Mac. Not with everyone nudging each other when they saw me and staring at me with knowing looks. I got on my bike and went down to Cremyll, where I sat on a bench and considered my options.

There wasn't too long to go now until the film wrapped here and the crew went up to London to shoot the scenes up there. The holidays were almost over. Was it worth going to Roland and begging for my job back as I still needed money for a camcorder? No way, I decided. He had made it very clear that he wanted me off the set. He hadn't liked me from day one. I could live without being involved in the last few days of the shoot, in fact, it would be cool to have a few days to myself. It bothered me that Charlie might think badly of me, though. I'd liked her. Maybe I'd drop her a line and put the record straight when it was all over.

Savannah and the photo? Just got to let that one go, I told myself. No doubt I'd be teased about it for months to come, but the gossip would die down in the end and it was a good lesson in how the press can make something out of nothing. Shame I never got to say goodbye to her, though. I really did think that we'd become friends. But that's another lesson, I told myself. Some people are like life: they take you up; they take you down.

And Lia? When I thought about Lia my stomach churned. But where it used to churn in a nice way when I thought about her, now the only sensation I felt was a knot of anxiety. Savannah, Charlie, the whole film set and everything that went with them would be up and gone in a few days. But Lia . . . She was a part of my life. I'd still see her every day at school. It had to be sorted, or seeing her would be a constant reminder of how things might have been if only I'd kept the promise I made to her that day on Whitsand beach. If only I'd told her about the rehearsal kiss. If only I could turn the clock back just a few days, we could maybe have had a laugh about it and she would still be my girlfriend.

This has to be one of the worst days of my whole life, I thought, as I sat there on the beach. I'd never felt so mixed up. I felt angry with Roland: sacking me had been so unfair.

I felt hurt by Savannah for taking off and leaving me in it, and without even saying goodbye. Not even a phone call. And, from the reactions of the crew that I'd seen this morning, not a word in my defence. She could have said something but it – or rather, I – obviously wasn't important enough for her to have taken the time out for.

I felt like a total reject. But there was still Lia. She hadn't rejected me; not yet. And maybe I could still rescue things with her. She was bound to see the newspaper sooner or later, but maybe if I came clean, apologised for not having told her about it, grovelled, begged, offered to carry her school books for the rest of eternity, she might give me a break. As my mum says, nothing is ever over until it's over.

I reached into my pocket, pulled out my mobile and tried Lia's mobile again. Still switched off, but this time I left a message for her: 'Lia, I really need to talk to you. Have you seen the paper today? There *is* an explanation. Call as soon as you get this message. Please.'

I waited at Cremyll for half an hour and watched as a couple of ferries came in and passengers got off. I felt numb, unsure what to do. Should I get on a ferry to Plymouth and go and look for Lia? Maybe not, I decided. For one thing, I didn't know where they'd have gone – they'd probably taken Donny to some posh place for lunch. Plus, there's no way I'd want him around when I see Lia. She'd probably have seen the paper by now and it would be so humiliating if she gave me the cold shoulder with Primadonny looking on. And if Lia's dad was there too . . . I like Zac Axford and we get on really well normally but he might not be so friendly if he thought I'd been cheating on his daughter.

I thought about going up to Lia's house and waiting by the gates. I'd get her on her own and explain everything. It was all innocent after all. But I couldn't get away from the nagging feeling in the pit of my stomach. The promise. The promise that we'd made to tell the truth to each other. I might be innocent as far as the kiss was concerned but I hadn't kept that promise. Promise to tell the truth, even if it hurts, no matter what. That's what she'd asked me.

I went home and luckily no one was there, as I didn't feel much like talking to anyone. Apart from Lia that is. I made a sandwich but I couldn't eat it. I went up to my room. It looked like a bomb had hit it – I hadn't tidied up since the beginning of the shoot. Half-heartedly, I began to put things away. Every fifteen minutes, I tried Lia's mobile. I didn't care if I seemed desperate. I wanted her to know how badly I wanted to get through to her.

Around one o'clock, I decided to phone her house and see if her mum had any idea when she might be home.

'Oh, they've just got back,' she said. 'Hold on, I'll call her.'

I felt my heart begin to thump in my chest as I waited for her to come to the phone. A few moments later, her mother came back on the line. 'Sorry, Squidge, she says she doesn't want to talk to you.'

'Oh, right,' I said. So that means she's seen the paper, I thought.

'Is something going on?' asked Mrs Axford, who clearly hadn't seen the paper but probably soon would.

'You could say that. Please tell Lia that I can explain everything. Please ask her to call.'

I put the phone down and stared at the wall. Then I stared at the phone and willed it to ring. Five minutes went by, ten minutes. Ring, ring, *please* ring, I thought. Maybe Lia had shown her mum the paper and they were all there calling me all the names under the sun. It felt awful to think that they'd all think so badly of me.

After half an hour, I couldn't stand it any more so I called Lia's mobile. Amazingly, this time, it wasn't switched off.

'Hello,' she said. I could tell instantly by her voice that she'd been crying.

'Lia, it's Squidge. Are you . . . Are you on your own?'

'Yes.'

'Lia, I can explain. That kiss – it was nothing. Savannah had to do the scene with Donny. A scene with kissing in it. She wanted to rehearse it and asked me to play Donny's part. There was nothing more to it than that, honestly. I didn't even want to do it, but how could I refuse?'

There was silence at the other end of the phone.

'Lia, *please* say something. I was going to tell you, I really was. I promise.'

'I . . . I can't believe your promises any more,' she said quietly.

'I know, I *know*,' I groaned. 'I know I should have told you before and I was going to. I tried to tell you that day I brought you the flowers, that day at Cremyll, but you looked so happy and we were having such a good time and I didn't want to ruin the moment. I guess I . . . I guess I chickened out.'

Again there was silence at Lia's end of the phone.

'Please Lia, say something.'

'Leave me alone,' she said. 'Just leave me alone. I don't want to see you any more. Just leave me alone.'

Then she hung up.

Hat-trick

A HAT-TRICK of rejections. I ought to get a prize, I thought as I rode up the windy lanes that led to Rame Head.

Fired by Roland.

Abandoned by Savannah.

Dumped by Lia.

That's three: a hat-trick. Mum's always saying that things come in threes so that's me done. And now I need to be on my own to look at the sky, or contemplate my navel, or whatever else it is you're supposed to do when life is grotty with a capital Grot.

Rame Head is one of my favourite places in the world. Not that I've travelled very far. But I reckon even when I have, I'll still treasure it. The actual spot is the ruin of a tiny church on top of a small hill on the peak of the Rame Peninsula. Once you've climbed up to the top, the view is astounding. Just sea and sky as far as the eye can see. But it's more than a beautiful location. There's a stillness up there. It makes me feel energised when I go there. If ever I feel low, I know half an hour up there and my battery will be recharged.

Once I got to the car park at the bottom of the hill, I locked my bike to the fence then climbed up to the ruined church. When I'd reached the top, I sat on the wall in front of the ruin and stared out to sea. This was the place that I'd brought Lia when we'd had our first kiss. It felt like a lifetime ago now. I knew that I'd blown it with her.

I'd never felt so low in my life. I'd tried to be everything to everyone. Tried to be the perfect boyfriend. Tried to be the perfect employee. Tried to be the perfect son. And where had it got me? On top of a hill, on my own, without a girlfriend, without a job and without enough money to replace the camcorder I broke. The fool on the hill. There was a song by the Beatles called that. Well, that's me, I thought: the fool on the hill.

I had a sudden urge to scream my head off. I'd read in one of Mum's mags about a therapy called primal scream therapy, where people do just that: scream their heads off. I remember thinking that it was a bonkers thing to do. But I didn't think that anymore. Not today. I took a quick peek down the hill to make sure I was all alone and wasn't going to scare some poor tourist stupid. Nope, no one on the horizon. I went back to my spot, took a deep breath and let it go:

'ArrrrrGHHHHHHHHHHHHHHHHHHHHHHHH
HHHHHHHHHHHHHHHHHHHHHHHHHHHHHHHH
HHHHHHHHHHHHHHHHHHHHHHHHHHHHHHHH
HHHHHHHHHHHHHHHHHHHHHHHHHHHHHHHH
HHHHHHHHHHHHHHH . . .'

I gulped in some air and let go again.

'ARRRRRRGGGGGGGGHHHHHHHHHHHHHHHHH
HHHHHHHHHHHHHHHHHHHHHHHHHHHHHHHH
HHHHHHHHHHHHHHHHHHHHHHHHHHHHHHHH
HHHHHHHHHHHHHHHHHHHHHHHHHHHHHHHH
HHHHHHHHHHHHHHHHHHHHHHHHHHHHHHHH
HHHHHHHHHHHHHHHHHHHHHHHHHHHHHHH.'

Suddenly the situation felt absurd and I started laughing and laughing. God, I really am the fool on the hill, I thought. If anyone saw me, they'd think I was totally mad. But somehow, the screaming did seem to have worked. I definitely felt better, like I'd released some of the tension from the past weeks. It was all fading away: Roland, Charlie, Savannah, Donny, Sandra, Chantelle, Martin Bradshawe – they'd all be gone soon and life in the Rame Peninsula would be back to normal. So my work experience had been a complete and utter disaster? So what? It wasn't the end of the world. School would be starting again. I could get my paper round back, finish saving up to replace the camcorder. Life would go on. Maybe I'd even tell Dad the truth about what had happened – that I'd fallen and damaged the lens. In fact, I don't know why I hadn't in the first place. He'd understand. He's cool, my dad, and he and Mum are always tripping over stuff that Amy has left lying around. These things happen. Things get broken. Nobody's perfect.

I just wished I hadn't lost Lia.

As I sat there, looking out to sea and thinking, one line kept going through my brain: everything passes, everything passes. Too right, I thought, as my eyes started to close, my limbs began to feel heavy and . . .

I must have nodded off because, the next thing I knew, someone was shaking my shoulder.

'Squidge, Squidge . . .'

It was Cat.

'Hey, what? Where . . .' I blustered.

She laughed. 'You've been asleep.'

'How did you know that I'd be here?'

'Where else would you be?' she smiled down at me. 'You always come here when things aren't working out for you and I know you've had a tough day.'

'That's an understatement.'

'You OK?'

I nodded. 'Yeah. Er, how long exactly have you been here?' I asked, panicking that she might have seen or heard my primal scream/maniacal laughter act.

'Just arrived.'

'Oh, so you didn't hear anything?'

'Like what?'

I glanced at my watch. I was amazed. I must have been asleep for over an hour. 'Oh, nothing.'

'So, is there anything I can do to help, Squidge?'

'Nah, just needed a bit of time by myself. You know, to think things over.'

'Do you want me to go?'

I shook my head. 'No, course not.'

'Heard you got fired.'

I nodded. 'And dumped. And abandoned.'

'Savannah?'

I nodded again. 'Apparently she's gone. I thought we were mates.'

She linked her arm through mine. 'No, *we're* mates,' she said. 'You and me and Mac and Becca and Lia.'

I smiled back at her. Dear old Cat. 'Not Lia, I don't think. I'm well in her bad books. Funny old business, isn't it?'

Just at that moment, my mobile bleeped. I took a quick look but didn't recognise the number. I saw that I had four missed calls. I must have missed them when I was yelling my head off or sleeping. No matter. I didn't want to speak to anyone apart from Lia and I'm sure she's not ready to talk to me again. Not yet.

'So, back to school soon,' said Cat.

'Yeah, I was just thinking that. The crew will all be gone and it will be like it was all a dream. Or a nightmare.'

'Was it how you expected?'

'Yes and no. I don't know what I expected. Maybe that everyone would be, I don't know, a bit nicer. I was so thrilled to be working on a film set. But, like anywhere, there are all sorts of people there: nice like Martin Bradshawe and nasty like Roland. I guess I've learned a lot in a way. I've learned to watch my back, that not everyone's on your side, just because you're all working on the same project . . .'

My mobile bleeped again.

'Aren't you going to answer that?' asked Cat.

I shook my head. 'I've been at everybody's beck and call for weeks now. If someone called, I jumped. And now it's back to my time again.'

'Might be Roland calling to apologise . . .'

I grimaced.

'OK, maybe not,' she said. 'Look, I'm starving. Let's go back to my house and grab something to eat. When the going gets tough, the tough have a good nosh.'

I laughed and suddenly realised that I hadn't eaten all day. 'Sounds great,' I said.

As we made our way back down to the village, with Cat on the back of my bike clinging to my waist, we saw Dad overtake us in his van. He stopped a few yards in front of us and leaped out.

'Where have you been?' he asked. 'Everyone's been looking for you. Don't you ever have your mobile switched on?'

'No, I mean, yes. Why? What's happened? Is Mum all right?'

'It's nothing like that. No, everyone's fine. Charlie Bennett's been looking for you. Something about locations and you being the only person who can help her.'

Cat raised an eyebrow and grinned.

'Here's the number she left,' said Dad, thrusting a piece of paper into my hand. 'She asked that you phone as soon as you can.'

'But I was fired,' I said.

'Think you might find that what Charlie wants has slightly more sway than Roland Rat,' said Cat.

'Yeah. Right. Course,' I said, dialling the number.

Charlie was hugely relieved when I got through to her.

'I need a beach where there's good access,' she said. 'The ones up at Whitsand are stunning, but no way can we get all the props and the lights and the cameras down those cliffs. I know there are beaches at Kingsand and Cawsand, but there are too many people around there, not to mention the boats and evidence of modern-day living. Can you think of anywhere else we could use?'

'Easy. You've got two choices,' I said. 'There's the beach down near Portwrinkle, it's just past the village at Crafthole on the left. Easy to get on to and not a café in sight. Or the beach out at Penlee Point. It's down below the ruin I showed you, to the left, kind of hidden away.'

'Excellent,' she said. 'I knew you'd come through. But where have you been? I looked everywhere at unit base, and Roland didn't seem to have any idea where you were.'

'I was sacked.'

There was silence at the other end. 'Roland?' she asked finally.

'Yep.'

'Well, you're hired again, that is if you'd like to be. Meet me at unit base in half an hour and we'll go out and check out Portwrinkle and Penlee Point.'

'Will do,' I said.

Cat laughed when I clicked my phone shut. 'The kid stays on the movie,' she said in a fake American accent, puffing on an imaginary cigar.

'Something like that,' I said, smiling back at her.

Velly Solly

CHARLIE WAS well pleased with the locations that I showed her and, spurred on by my change of fortune, I decided to come clean with Dad about the camcorder as soon as I got home that evening.

He was totally cool about it.

'Could happen to anyone in this house,' he said as he watched Amy trying to force feed mashed potato to her teddy bear. 'I only wish you'd told me about it at the time. I could have got cousin Ed to sort it.'

'I didn't want you to think that I was a total prat,' I said. 'You know, breaking my new toy on the first day.'

'No worries,' said Dad, then he laughed. 'I already think that you're a total prat so no change there.'

'Thanks, Dad,' I grinned back at him. I knew what he'd said was his strange way of telling me that it was OK.

After supper, I charged upstairs and dialled Lia's number. Hopefully, my new run of luck will extend to getting back with her, I thought as I crossed my fingers and prayed.

Sadly that idea was a no go as she wouldn't take my call.

'I suppose you could try flowers again,' said Becca, when we met in the catering tent the next day. 'She was bowled over last time.'

I shook my head. 'Been there, done that.'

'Chocolates,' said Mac.

'A love poem,' suggested Cat.

'Me am Squidge, am full of folly,' Mac began. 'Messed things up, am velly solly.'

'Very romantic. Not,' I said. I was grateful for their support, though. At least they were still my mates, and even though Becca had been a bit sniffy with me at first, after she'd given me the third degree over the kiss with Savannah, she'd decided that I wasn't a rat after all.

'I could write a love song for her,' suggested Becca.

'*Noooo*,' we all chorused. Her songs are worse than Mac's poems though no one's had the nerve to actually tell her truth about them.

'Why not?' she asked.

'Er . . . It ought to come from me,' I said, then I looked at Cat. 'Or maybe not. You could help if you would, Cat.'

'Sure,' she said.

'Tell her that you believe me. And Becca, and Mac – tell her again that the kiss was part of a rehearsal. Explain that it meant nothing.'

Cat rolled her eyes. 'Do me a favour. I told her all *that* yesterday.'

'So why is she still not talking to me?'

'She said something about not being able to trust you and trust being the most important thing in a relationship. Something about a promise you made her.'

I sighed. 'I know, I blew it over that. But she can trust me.'

'She said that it wasn't the fact that you kissed Savannah and that it was on the front cover. She said it was the fact that you didn't tell her about it and that she was the last person in Cornwall to find out. Made her look like a prat, she said.'

I winced. That must have been tough for her and there was nothing I could say in my defence. I remembered what I had told her about people only withholding facts from each other when there's something to hide, or when there's something going on that they didn't want the other person to know about. And I hadn't told her about the rehearsal or the photo. I'd hidden it from her. It's weird, I thought. The two times I've withheld information in order to protect someone are the two times things have gone really wrong for me. First not wanting to upset Dad by telling him that I'd damaged my new camcorder. If only I'd been honest about it, it might have got sorted with Cousin Ed, end of story. Instead I got the job as a runner to pay for its repair and managed to get myself into a right mess. And second not telling Lia that Savannah had asked me to do the rehearsal with her. We'd promised to tell each other the truth, no matter what. Hah! I'd had the opportunity to come clean, but I hadn't because I didn't want to ruin her day. But by holding out, I'd ended up hurting her more.

'You need to do something really cool,' said Cat. 'Not the usual flowers and pressies. Do a Squidge. Something unique. Anybody can buy her stuff.'

'Yeah,' said Mac with a cheeky grin. 'Do a Dawson.'

I smacked him lightly on the arm and the girls looked at us quizzically. 'Private joke,' I said. 'But good idea, Cat. Do something unique. But what?'

'I know,' said Mac. 'Last Christmas, when I asked my gran what she wanted as a present, she said that at her time of life she had all the nick-nacks she wanted and that she could buy herself anything else that she fancied. She said the nicest thing to get is an experience.'

'Like what?' asked Becca. 'A night with a stripper?'

Mac laughed. 'Nah, a night with a stripper at my gran's age might kill her off. No, mum booked her a facial and I got her a manicure.'

'So what you're saying is that I should call up Lia and apologise again, then ask if she wants her nails doing?'

'No, dufus,' said Mac. 'Nothing like that. You'll think of something.'

We sat there for a while, chatting about what I could do. Then suddenly, I had an idea.

'This just might work,' I said.

It was all arranged for the following night.

First I sent Lia a handmade invite, with a picture of an orchid that I'd cut out of a magazine, in the corner.

You are invited to a private showing of Sleepless in Seattle.
Place: Squidge's back garden
Time: Saturday at 9.30
Dress: Casual

Sleepless in Seattle was Lia's favourite film. I hired it from the video shop. After that I went shopping for all Lia's favourite movie food: Haagen Daz pecan fudge icecream, butterscotch popcorn and plenty of elderflower cordial. When I got home, Mac came over and helped me with the garden. I got out all the Christmas lights and arranged them over bushes and trees so that the garden looked like fairy land. The unusually warm weather that we were having was still with us, and with a bit of luck it would hold for one more night.

Dad thought I was mad, but when Mum found out what the plan was she thought it was lovely. 'It's going to look sooooo romantic,' she sighed. 'How will Lia be able to resist?'

Dad, Mac and Will helped me shift furniture. Putting old cushions out on the lawn and blankets, in case it got chilly later on. We moved the TV and video machine to the French windows, so that they faced into the garden. The last touch was to line the path with night lights in brown paper bags from the green grocers, weighed down with soil from the flower beds. They looked great, like Japanese lanterns. Cat and Becca offered to act as usherettes. They dressed in black trousers, white shirts and baseball caps so that they looked like they had a uniform on. I showered, changed, slapped on some of Dad's Armani, and I was ready.

The stage was set.

The lights were lit.

Mum and Dad had gone next door with Amy to have a drink with a neighbour.

My brother, Will, stayed behind and was ready with the torch to show Lia to her place.

Becca was ready with the ice cream.

Cat was ready with chocs, popcorn and drinks.

There was only one person missing . . .

Lia.

Nine thirty passed. Ten o'clock. Ten fifteen.

'She's not coming, guys,' I said, finally. 'Might as well crack open the ice cream. No point in wasting it.'

Cat and Becca did their best to console me. Even Mac and Will had a go at cheering me up, by offering to light their farts, but I wasn't in the mood. I'd blown it, all by breaking my promise to tell the truth, no matter what. I felt rotten. The truth no matter what. At the time of making the promise, I could never in my wildest dreams have imagined that the no matter what was going to be a snog with one of the most famous teen stars in the world. Even so, the bottom line was that I'd broken my promise and lost Lia.

16 Lights, Camera, Action

WE WERE ABOUT to start the video when at ten thirty, the doorbell rang.

Will ran through the house and peeked through the front window. He ran back.

'It's Lia,' he whispered. 'Shall I let her in?'

'Yeah, course,' I said.

Will ran back into the sitting room, then turned and ran back to us. 'Shall I give her the torch treatment?'

The doorbell rang again. 'Yeah, course, the full works, but *hurry* or else she'll think that there's no one here and go home.'

Will went and turned the electric light off in the hall, switched on his torch and opened the front door. A few minutes later, he led a rather bewildered looking Lia through into the garden.

'Wow,' she said when she saw the set up. 'It's like Santa's Christmas grotto.'

It was brilliant to see her. She looked stunning as always, with her hair loose down her back. But I could see that her face looked strained, like she'd been crying. It was obvious that she'd been going through it as well.

Cat and Becca sprang out from behind the rhododendron bush. 'Would madam like some refreshments?' asked Becca. 'We have the finest quality popcorn.'

'Or chocolate,' said Cat. 'At least what's left of it. I'm afraid we ate all the ice cream.'

'What's going on?' Lia asked. 'What's everyone doing here?'

'Private showing of *Sleepless in Seattle*. As it said on your invite.'

Lia smiled at the others. 'Doesn't look very private to me.'

'Everyone wanted to pitch in. I'm so glad you came . . .'

'I wasn't going to. I . . . I've been sitting at home . . .'

'But you *did* come . . . I . . .'

Lia nodded. 'I wanted to talk to you.'

I wished the others would go away for a few minutes. We needed to be on our own. But they were all there, like they were rooted to the ground, first listening to what I said, then to Lia, then to me, their heads turning my way then hers, like they were watching a tennis match and we were the players.

For a few moments, there was a strained silence.

Finally Will sighed tragically. 'Remind me never to have girlfriend,' he said. '*Way* too much hassle.'

Lia laughed and the ice was broken.

'I'm so glad you came,' I said. 'I know *Sleepless in Seattle* is your favourite movie. And,' I indicated the lights and everything, 'I wanted to make it special.'

'And we all wanted to help,' said Cat. 'Because it's mad that you two aren't getting on when you're clearly crazy about each other.'

'Crazy's the word,' said Will, rolling his eyes.

Lia shifted her feet awkwardly and I grinned at her like an idiot. She was here. Was there hope after all?

'Would you like five minutes alone?' asked Mac.

We both nodded.

'OK,' said Becca, 'but *then* can we watch the movie?'

Mac punched her lightly on the arm.

'*Ow*,' she groaned. Mac pushed her inside and Cat grabbed Will and hoisted him in after them.

Lia and I were alone at last.

'About the . . .' we both said at the same time.

'No, you go,' we both said, again at the same time. Then

we laughed. 'You first,' we said, again together. Then we both laughed again.

'So,' I said.

'So,' said Lia.

'Er,' I said.

'Um,' said Lia.

'It's like . . .' I said.

'I know,' said Lia.

'I'm really, really, really sorry.'

Lia looked at the grass. 'So am I. I've missed you. I've been sitting up at the house feeling miserable and wanting to call, wondering if it was too late and you hated me, then I thought . . .'

'And I've been sitting here waiting for you, thinking that I'd blown it, cursing myself for being so stupid . . .'

'So it's not too late?'

'Your call,' I said. 'It was me who broke the promise and I . . .'

Lia put a finger over my lips and shook her head. I got it: no need for words, no more apologies. Then, at the same time, we both moved towards each other for a great movie-style kiss.

'Can we come back now?' Becca called through the French windows five minutes later. 'As we take it from the snogging marathon that things are OK between you.'

'No, they're not,' I said. 'We're still not speaking.'

Lia laughed. 'No, we only speak the language of lurve.'

'Oh, vomit,' said Becca, flouncing through the doors and flopping herself down on one of the beanbags. She lay there for a minute and looked up at the sky. 'Fab night. All the stars are out.'

Cat, Mac and Will came into the garden and flopped down next to her.

'After you, madam,' I said to Lia.

'No, after you,' she said.

'No, after you,' I said.

'Oh, for God's sake stop being so nice to each other and sit down,' said Becca.

We did as we were told.

'Look at the stars,' commanded Becca.

Again, we did as we were told and all lay back and stared up into the night sky.

It was a clear night, with every star in the galaxy twinkling as if competing for the Star of the Year competition. As I lay there – my mates on either side, my hand in Lia's – I felt happier than I had for weeks, for months. Looking up at the vast canopy above me, I thought, these stars, these same stars, look down on Hollywood and they look down here on Cawsand village. You can fence off the world with maps – saying this is America and this is England and this is Europe – but who is going to do that to the sky that exists over it all, without fence, without border, without perimeter? I sighed a sigh of deep contentment. So I lived in the Rame peninsula, in some Cornish backwater, but up there were the stars and they twinkled to me that there were other locations waiting under their gaze for me to discover. But for now, I lived in a great place, with a great family and I had great friends. The future was looking good. Charlie had said I could look her up for a job when I left film school. She'd even made Roland write me a top reference for my CV! I was back with Lia. And life under the stars, as opposed to working with them (or snogging them), was good.

'Ready, everyone?' I asked.

'Ready,' they all chorused back.

I picked up the remote. 'Right. Lights, camera, action.' I pressed the remote and the movie started to play. Lia snuggled down in my arms, Becca curled up with Mac and Will looked hopefully at Cat.

'In your dreams, matie,' she said.

'One day, you'll regret this,' he said. 'I may be young but I'm very experienced.'

That set us all off laughing. It felt great. Perfect mates, in a perfect location, on a perfect evening. It might be fun making movies, I thought but it's even more fun watching them.

If you would like more information about
books available from Piccadilly Press and how
to order them, please contact us at:

Piccadilly Press Ltd.
5 Castle Road
London
NW1 8PR

Tel: 020 7267 4492
Fax: 020 7267 4493

Feel free to visit our website at
www.piccadillypress.co.uk